SECOND
Chance

JOSEPH GRANDE

ARCHWAY
PUBLISHING

Archway Publishing books may be ordered through booksellers or by contacting:

Archway Publishing
1663 Liberty Drive
Bloomington, IN 47403
www.archwaypublishing.com
844-669-3957

ISBN: 978-1-6657-2318-3 (sc)
ISBN: 978-1-6657-2319-0 (e)

Library of Congress Control Number: 2022908327

Print information available on the last page.

Archway Publishing rev. date: 06/07/2022

Dedicated with love to the original 7.

CONTENTS

CHAPTER 1

ANOTHER BEAUTIFUL MIAMI SUNSET, WARM BEACHES, ANOTHER day in paradise. We hear a woman giggling in a very seductive manner. Paige, a beautiful young woman in her early twenties, is dressed in a sheer clinging red dress. Sprawled on a couch, she has a faraway look about her as she leans over a black granite table to slowly snort a line of cocaine. She yells, "Cooper, were you on the phone?" Cooper is a tall, good-looking, very tanned guy. As he turns around to make sure Paige is not coming into the room, he continues the conversation in a very low and controlled voice, "8:30 to Paris confirmed, thank you." Cooper has always taken pride in his appearance and today was no different with his tailored suit, which fits his large frame like a glove. He possesses a controlled, emotionless look. Paige yells, "Cooper, where are we going tonight?" He stands up with fixed eyes darting in every direction; suddenly, his face changes. Cooper enters the living room, where Paige looks up at him in anticipation like a star just entered the room. His features are now full of smiles. He enters the room with a few small packages in his hands. Paige looks and screams, "Wow! Are they for me?" "Be patient baby, who else would they be for?" "Give them to me now, please." As she continues to beg for them, he convinces her to wait until they make a quick stop. "You know how it is business before pleasure, come baby, we don't want to be late. Pick up all of your goodies, and let's get going." Paige slowly starts to pick up all her paraphernalia while Cooper watches observantly. He takes his handkerchief and makes sure the table is clean. He then looks around to make sure nothing is out of place. They leave and go downstairs and get into

Cooper's parked car. He opens the passenger door to make sure that Paige gets in, "You really can act strange sometimes." He ignores her, gets in the driver's seat, starts the car, and begins to drive away while Paige is checking her makeup. Out of the clear blue sky, she remarks, "Let me tell you about this dream I had last night." Cooper, whose intense self-questioning eyes continue to monitor the road ahead, does not pay much attention to her as Paige's voice recedes, becoming inaudible, and just the purr of the engine can be heard. A few minutes later, Cooper pulls up in front of an isolated warehouse—god knows where—and climbs out. Paige looks out and says, "Where the hell are we Cooper?" She opens the car window and asks, "Can I come along with you? You never let me come along." Cooper tries to keep his good luck going, smiles in a very non-descriptive manner, and answers, "Sure baby, why not." Paige is surprised and leaps out of the car without hesitation. Cooper grabs her hand and leads her to the entrance of the warehouse. He unlocks the door, and they both enter hand in hand. It's dark, moldy, and smells of rotten eggs. Cooper walks across the room while Paige waits in anticipation as he switches on a light. It is so dreary that Paige scurries to his side and clings to his arm. He turns and tells her to relax, as there are no ghosts. Cooper removes her grip on his arm and motions to her to wait as he walks over to a dusty table in the middle of the room. He places two packages on the tabletop. He turns and feels that she is at his disposal. He turns toward the table, picks up one of the boxes, and starts to remove the contents of the box – clothes. He asks her to put them on. Paige looks puzzled, "What? You want me to put these on? You want to please me, don't you baby?" A sigh of relief passes over her, and she starts to undo her dress. She takes the straps off her shoulders, and her dress sinks to the floor. She stands there with this innocent look running her hands up and down her sides. Cooper lets out a gasp with his animal instinct, and his imagination starts to run wild. "What a body, baby, wow!" She continues and puts on the shirt overalls but hesitates when she looks at the ugly boots that he hands her. "Who am I? What am I supposed to be? I do not get it." Cooper replies, "You're asking too many questions. Just do this for me, or you are going to spoil the surprise. He angrily walks to the other end of the warehouse and flicks another light along the wall. You can see twenty or more barrels. He slowly walks over and places one of the packages on top of them. As he turns, he says, "Paige baby, I have something special for you tonight." Her face lights up, and a look of satisfaction engulfs her as she gingerly moves to the table. Like a kid in a candy store, she waits for her surprise. Cooper reaches into his pocket, removes a vial, and hands it to her. "Enjoy, baby." She smiles and pulls out her mirror, pours out the white powder she lives for, and takes two large snorts. She smiles, and her world is full of dreams and good times. "Wow, this was worth waiting for. It's the best I have ever had, thank you baby!" He leans close to her and whispers in her ear for several minutes. Her mouth opens wide, and her eyes widen as she turns toward Cooper, who grabs her by the shoulder. Paige screams angrily and demands to know why her face is frozen. As she gasps for air, holding her eyes peer into nothingness, she twitches. Cooper leans close and whispers again. Her convulsions disappear, and her head slowly drops sideways onto her mirror. Her gasping breath barely fogs the mirror. Cooper, with his look of supreme power, gives her a kiss. Her face still has a tiny twitch near the bottom lip. The fogging area shrinks and finally vanishes. Her struggle ends. Cooper, with a smile, lifts her head off the mirror, pulls away the mirror with the powder, and gently places her back on the table. Cooper stands straight up again with his usual confident smile and remarks, "It's done." A change overcomes him. His smile turns into a blank face—the same face we saw the first time we met him: emotionless, calm, and confident. He removes her jewelry with the precision of a surgeon and places it in his pocket. He puts on a mask, walks over to the barrels, and begins to tilt them over with passion and glee on his face. The fluid from the barrels quickly reaches Paige's limp body. Cooper looks around and exits the warehouse with a smirk on his face. He closes the door behind him and makes sure the lock is securely on. He walks over to his parked car, stops, pauses as he senses the night air, takes a deep breath, and yells, "All is well, life is good." He then climbs into his car. He notes the time, starts the engine, pauses to open his glove compartment, and pulls out his passport and airline ticket to Paris. He lays them gently on the passenger seat and slowly drives away into the night. He is only a few hundred yards down the road, but it feels like an eternity to him. He boldly gets out of his car, and with an air of confidence, reaches into his pocket and pulls out his cell phone. He dials some numbers and, without hesitation, sends the signal. Within seconds, the warehouse is engulfed in a large ball of fire, and an explosion occurs like bombs exploding in a war zone. He does not flinch, but simply gets back into his car and drives away, turning on his radio like he is out for a Sunday drive. All you can hear is the sound of the car muffler slowly fading into the night.

CHAPTER 2

ONE YEAR LATER, IN A QUIET NEIGHBORHOOD WITH PASTEL-COLORED HOUSES, PALM TREES, AND A SLEEPY AMBIANCE, WE SEE several men huddled against the only three-story red brick building in the area. It seems out of place, like it belongs in New York City, not Miami. They go up the stairs quietly, with their guns in hand, caution in their approach, and apprehension with each step they take. After climbing two floors up to apartment 211, the tension is broken when one of the officers drops a very loud fart. Everyone snickers covering their faces, momentarily distracting them from the task – a tension breaker for the moment. As they position themselves around the door, Officer Scott kicks in the door with such force that the lock falls off with the impact. They bust through the door like a precision drill team. To their amazement, the occupants seem in a daze and are not impressed. One guy is half asleep, lying on the couch in his underwear, sipping a beer. He then suddenly realized what had just happened. They are all awakened from their dreams with a look of panic and start to run in all directions, just like the first fire drill in kindergarten, when you know you are scared but have no idea where to go, so you just start to run. Officer Scott, realizing the situation, screams at the top of his voice, "Shut the fuck up and freeze." Officer Scott approaches a closed door and opens it slowly. To his surprise, he sees two people getting it on and completely unaware of what just happened in the apartment. From a moment of pleasure to a moment of panic, they finally realize that they have company. The woman is a skinny blonde girl who looks very young. She is skinny as a rail but has the biggest set of breasts that a local plastic surgeon would have created. Both panic, and the man throws her off him. She lands on the floor next to the bed. She screams, "You son of a bitch. Why did you do that?" "Stupid bitch, don't you realize we have company in the room?" As Officer Scott approaches the love birds, the man starts to scream, "She is old enough, she is eighteen, she is eighteen, don't shoot." Suddenly, his fear turns to anger, and he starts to scream at the top of his voice, "Can a guy get laid these days without interruption?" He finally realizes that the intruder is a policeman and asks him what he is doing there. Officer Scott loudly tells him to shut up and get dressed. He puts on his underwear, and Officer Scott cuffs him and pushes him to the side. "Let's go sunshine, we don't have all day." The blond puts on her clothes, and she also gets cuffed. Office Scott screams, "One of you guys take care of the love birds." As he passes by the open window in the room, he notices one of the occupants of the apartment running down the street for his life. He screams to Officer Lisa, "I will get that son of a bitch", and starts his pursuit of the perpetrator, unaware that another officer is flush against the building down the street waiting for his change to get in on the action. As the perpetrator nears the area, Officer Scott and the hidden officer collide with the perpetrator like a train wreck. With Officer Dean smiling over the shadow, not realizing that he knocked down the perpetrator, and with Officer Scott being slow-footed, taking advantage of the situation, the perpetrator gets up and starts to run again. Both the officers look at each other in disbelief, "You stupid fuck, I should have known it was you." They both get up and start the chase again, realizing that to cut him off, they need a little luck and a better plan to recapture the perpetrator. As Officer Scott turns the corner, gasping for air, to his surprise, he watches the suspect with his hands in the air backing away. As he gets closer, he sees Officer Dean with his weapon in hand, screaming at the suspect to stop. With both of them gasping for air and lucky to have caught him, Officer Dean screams out, "Cuff that piece of shit and read him his rights." As Officer Dean slumps over trying to catch his breath, the suspect turns around and knocks Officer Dean to the ground with a swift kick to the back of his leg, dropping his weapon to the ground. The suspect reaches, picks up his .38 special, and motions to Officer Scott to stay still. With a smile, he remarks, "Who is the piece of shit now?" Officer Scott is so pissed off at this situation and has all the intentions of reaching for his weapon. Officer Dean begs him to stay cool, as it appears the suspect has made fools out of both of them. Officer Scott reluctantly and slowly takes his weapon out of his holster and throws it to the ground. As Officer Dean is slowly getting on his feet, he screams out to the suspect, "You asshole! You made a big mistake." With a crazed look in his eyes, he starts to walk toward the suspect. Officer Scott stands there in disbelief. Officer Dean continues to walk toward the suspect and screams, "I don't want to shoot you stupid fuck, but I will, without hesitation, if I have to." Officer Dean continues toward him. The look on the faces of Officer Scott and the suspect is like "What the hell is going on? Does he have a death wish?" Out of sheer panic, the suspect fires a round point-blank. Officer Dean keeps walking toward the perp. Another round is discharged, and Officer Dean is still on his feet. The suspect yells, "You must be Superman. No person should still be on his feet after they have been shot twice." Dazed and confused, the suspect is frozen in space. Officer Dean kicks the suspect in the groin, and he falls to the ground. With his face white as snow, he screams, "How can this fuck still be standing." Officer Scott, in disbelief on his face and confused with what he just witnessed, grabs the gun away from the suspect and while standing over him repays him with a few more kicks to the groin, "Paybacks are hell, brother." Officer Dean leans over and picks up Officer Scott's 38 special. The perpetrator starts to complain about stomach pains, and Officer

Dean remarks, "What do you suppose is wrong with him?" Officer Scott shrugs his shoulder, "I don't know. These guys are always crying wolf police brutality. Oh yeah, you better read him his rights again and walk him toward the other officers." Officer Dean reaches into his pocket, pulls out a lighter, and lights up a cigarette. He takes a long hard drag, coughs, walks away, stops, looks back down the street, and laughs to himself, "It was just a fucking hundred yards, and it almost killed me running after him. It seemed like a hundred years ago that I could run all day long without losing my lunch. I better start getting in better shape." Officer Scott pushes the suspect in the back of the patrol car and, like a hungry lion, looks around to see where Officer Dean is. He runs over to him, grabs him by the collar, and starts to choke him. They both fall to the ground, and Officer Dean screams, "Let go, I will explain it to you. Give me a chance." They both stand up, and Officer Scott screams, "Start you stupid fuck, and you better be convincing." Dean tells him that he is involved in a local actors' playhouse, and he is the detective in the show. He forgot to switch the blanks out of his service revolver. "You could have gotten us both killed you stupid dumb fuck! From now on, I don't want you to ever talk to me, and if I see you around me, I will kill you myself." He gets into his car and starts to drive to the police station. As he arrives at the station, he looks around and thinks, "This place looks more like a cheap boarding house than a police station." Officer Dean opens the front door and walks in, only to see Garcia, the front desk Sergeant, with a very big smile on his face. He remarks, "How are you doing superman," and starts to laugh out loud. Officer Dean turns around, flips him the bird, and continues to walk through the double doors to the detective room. As the guys see him, the fun begins. They start to laugh so hard that they fall to their knees. As he passes by each of them, they ask, "Did you remind yourself to put real bullets in your gun today?" "I am not sure, let me check." "How about you, Brian?

Not really, he is laughing so hard that he can hardly speak." Dean turns around, points his arms in the air like he is conducting an orchestra, and tells them all to go fuck themselves. He realizes that the same guys who were rolling all over the floor only a moment ago are now scurrying to their desks like a bunch of wild dogs. Dean continues to conduct the boys, not realizing that the boss, Captain Flynn, a robust 45-year-old seasoned police officer, is standing behind him with his arms crossed and an angry look on his face screaming, "What in hell is going on in here?" Officer Dean finally realizes what is going on and turns around, only to hear the boss scream, "You stupid son of a bitch. Get in my office right now." As he slowly walks into the Captain's office, Officer Scott is already sitting in front of the Captain's desk. He starts to say to the Captain, "I thought it was over today. This stupid son of a bitch has been making B movies for a so-called friend named Grace." "Listen, you fat slob. I don't like the tone of your voice when you talk about Grace." "Stop it," screams Captain Flynn, "I want to hear this story." Dean continues, and you shut your mouth." Like I was saying, I help Grace make films about police work, and in some of the takes, we use blanks in the gun." "You mean your gun?" "Yes sir", Scott continues "and today, lover boy forgot to put the real thing in his gun, and when push came to shove, I thought it was all over for me Captain." "You have to straighten this shit out. I can't work with this mental case anymore." Captain Flynn turns around and screams out, "Is this true?" Officer Dean nods his head. "You are crazier than I thought, and you, Officer Scott, do not make out a report until you talk to me. Do you understand me, do you?" "Yes, sir." "Get the fuck out of my office. I do not want to see your ugly face around here until I call you." "Yes sir." "And as for you stupid bastard, tomorrow, your first act is to report to the police shrink without hesitation, do you understand me or do I have to make it any clearer than that? I will make all the arrangements. And by the way, the detectives' promotion list came out today, and your fucking name was on it. "Who the fuck do you have pictures on?" screams Officer Scott. "I have been trying to make Sergeant for the past six years, and they go and promote this mental case. Your father must be turning over in his grave right now." "Get out of my face and consider yourself on vacation until I call you. Do you understand that?" "Yes sir." "Now both of you get out of this office before I use real bullets on both of you."

Captain Flynn realizes that the situation with Officer Dean must be resolved. It had been a few weeks since the encounter in his office. He shouts, "Mary," and she finally answers him, "Yes, Captain?" "Call that so-called Officer Dean and tell him to be in my office bright and early on Wednesday at 9 a.m., and if he is late, to look for another job. Make that very clear to him." Mary gets up from her desk and slowly opens her office door. She walks down the long hallway toward the detective's room and opens the door. All eyes were glued on her. Once you look at Mary, you have to understand the Latino heatwave. With the body she has, you have dreams that never materialize, and then you wake up. She walks in slowly, looks around, and begins to ask, "Has anyone heard from Officer Dean?" They all started to snicker. "Are you kidding Mary? That guy is bad luck." One of the guys hears Mary's request and politely starts to wave his hand to get her attention. As she looks over, he whispers, "I am talking to him on the phone." She motions to him that when he is finished, she would like to speak to him. He nods his head in affirmation. He tells Dean that Mary is waiting to speak to him, and Dean asks if she is still pissed off at him. He replies that it is something that he is going to have to ask her himself. Mary, standing close to the detective, overhears the remark, takes the phone, and replies to Dean, "You can't imagine what this place has been like since you pulled off that dumb stunt." Mary explains Captain Flynn's instructions to Dean, and he replies with his usual cavalier attitude, "I will be in with bells on," and Mary replies, "For your own good, leave that attitude at home because the mood here is your balls will be cut off." "Mary, I love when you talk dirty." "So long, jerk."

CHAPTER 3

THE ALARM RINGS AND THE DAY OF RECKONING HAS ARRIVED. Dean slams the top of the alarm clock in disgust, knowing what he had to face today. Slowly, he gets up and heads toward the bathroom. Still in a daze, he stops to shave. After finishing, he steps in the shower, dries off, and wanders down the hallway toward the bedroom. He realizes that he has nothing to wear, as most of the time on the force he has been undercover, and the last time he wore a suit was for his mother's funeral. Out of nowhere, tears run down his face as he remembers his mother. He reluctantly opens the closet door and starts to rummage through the few clothes hanging in the closet. He finds the only suit: the black double-breasted. He thinks to himself, "Another funeral, this time may be my own. I hope that this time the results are far better than before. The way I look, it should even impress the old goat." He finishes dressing and starts to make his way downstairs. He opens the front door and walks to his car, parked in the driveway. He takes a deep breath and remarks, "Let's get this over with." He opens the door to his car, starts it up, and starts driving to the police station, as usual. When he arrives, it's hell trying to park the car unless you are on duty; otherwise, it's around the block a few times until you finally find a parking space, and it's at least a block away. He gets out of the car and slowly starts to walk to the police station. When he finally arrives at the front door, he opens the door, and Garcia, the front desk Sergeant, starts to whistle at him, "Oh baby, you look marvelous! What part are you playing today?" and breaks out in a deep belly laugh. Dean turns around and blows him a kiss as he walks by heading toward Captain Flynn's office. As usual, there are always a few detectives milling around. Upon seeing Dean all cleaned up, they start with their cat calls and throw him kisses. He tries to ignore them but finally turns around and flips them the bird. It seems like an eternity, but finally, he arrives at Captain Flynn's office door. However, first, he makes sure that he looked good and presentable. He knocks on the door and waits to be invited in. As usual, the loud voice of the boss calls out to come on in. Captain Flynn raises his eyes and asks Officer Dean to sit down. As Flynn starts to speak, Officer Dean interrupts him. The Captain stops him and replies in a low voice, "I do not want to hear any of your bullshit stories. Dean is surprised to hear the low voice, as he is not accustomed to it coming from him. "Do you understand me?" "Yes sir." "Listen to me and listen good. I will not repeat myself. From now on, you will be working for me and no one else. Do we understand each other?" Dean replies, "Yes sir."

"This is the scenario. In the past few years, we have been getting reports of more than a few mysterious explosions throughout the city, resulting in more and more bodies appearing, or what was left of them, and the Mayor is putting pressure on me to solve this problem. This is where you come in, genius. The reports of these incidents are all over local newspapers and TV stations, and everyone is screaming for solutions to the problem. For your information, sport, bits and pieces of your last girlfriend have been identified by the forensic department."

Dean was caught off guard, and in a crackly voice, he replies, "Holy shit! She told me she was moving back to New York to her sister's place, that lying piece of shit!" Captain Flynn replies, "I see you really have a way with women. Maybe this will give you an incentive to get your shit together". He said that she was not that important to him. "Captain, Paige was just another girl, oh, but you can still remember her name tough guy. I am going to give you a special assignment, and if anyone, and I mean anyone, hears about it, your ass will be out of this department." He loudly repeats as he gets up from his desk with papers in his hand, "Do I make myself clear? Do you know what these are?" Flickering the papers in his hand, he growls at Dean, "They are your future hot shot. One more fuck up, and your ass is gone." "What are they," asks Dean. "Your resignation forms. Do I make myself clear?" "Yes sir."

Too stupid to realize it, later that afternoon, sitting in his living room thinking of the events of the day, he hears the phone ringing in the kitchen. He gets up and runs to answer it, thinking it's Grace calling to apologize, but it's a strange voice at the other end. "Mr. Dean, this is Dr. Abbey Fernandez' office. You were referred to us by Captain Flynn. Hold on, and the doctor will explain the situation to you. Hold on as I connect you with the doctor." A few moments passed that seemed like hours. Finally, there was a voice at the other end, "Good afternoon, this is Dr. Abbey Fernandez. I hope I did not catch you at a bad time." "Not at all, just surprised." Dr. Abbey Fernandez goes on to explain to Dean that Captain Flynn called and made her aware of your past situation and asked me to help you. Let's get started as soon as possible." Dean is surprised and bewildered with the phone call. Dean asks the doctor how long this was going to take. "Mr. Dean, therapy is not like going to the supermarket. It's going to take time to get into your real problems." "But doctor I don't have a problem." "Let me be the judge of that. I will put my receptionist on the phone so that you can start making appointments. Have a good day, and please hold." A few minutes go by, and finally the receptionist gets on the phone. "Mr. Dean let's start your appointments on Monday at 9:00. Is that ok with you?" "Sure." "Do you have a paper and pencil ready for noting down our address? It's 45 Collins. Are you familiar with Collins? It is in South Beach. Are you familiar with that area?" "Yes, I am." "Then we will see you on Monday at 9:00 am sharp. Thank you and have a nice day." He hangs up the phone, and his head is still spinning. He thinks to himself, "What the hell just happened?" He became confused, "That son of a bitch thinks I am nuts. Who does he think he is?" He is so mad he can hardly see the numbers on the phone and dials Captain Flynn. The phone rings and rings, and finally he hears a familiar voice on the phone, "Captain Flynn's office, how may I help you?" "You can put that crazy bastard on the phone." Mary, realizing Dean's tone of voice, tries to calm him down and rapidly asks Dean to calm down. "Let him explain it to you as you know why he had to do this." "How in hell do you know about this Mary?" "Well, stupid, I made the initial phone call to set up the appointment for you. Hold on, I will transfer you to his phone." Mary rings the extension, and you hear Flynn's loud voice, "Captain Flynn speaking, how can I help you?" Dean screams, "How can you help me by sending me to a shrink? What are you doing to me Captain?" "Listen, son, please calm down, and I will explain it to you. First take a deep breath and listen." It was strange for Dean to hear that much compassion from the old goat, but finally, he realized that he should hear his side of the story. "Now look back on your police career, and you will see you haven't been the postcard of a perfect policeman. You always made things hard for yourself because of your poor attitude. Well, your last stunt was the last straw. You either do exactly as you are told for once in your life, or I can't help you. You were born with a gold star up your ass. Not only did you put yourself in danger, but everyone on the team. Now listen, you stupid fuck and listen well. Get all the help that Dr. Fernandez can give you, talk things out, listen for once without any trouble, and report to me on a weekly basis. But that does not excuse you from the job I gave you. You are the luckiest man alive, Dean. God must have been sitting on the detective promotion board because a fuck-up like you gets promoted. To this day, I don't know how it happened. You must have pictures of the board members, and by the way, genius, when Dr. Abbey Fernandez gives you the green light, which is when you will officially call yourself a detective. God help us all. Good luck!" A new start. As he thinks about a new beginning, he starts to talk to himself, "Get yourself together! Talk to the shrink! Get yourself straight and give Dr. Abbey Fernandez and yourself a chance to really see what's wrong with you."

As Dean looks back, it seems like only yesterday, and here it is. "Four months had passed, and thinking back, the therapy was lively, enthusiastic, and, most of all, helpful. I finally realized that I was really carrying a huge burden on my shoulders all along. The four months of therapy with Dr. Abbey Fernandez turned out to be a good thing and was the first step for me to look at life in a new light. The last thing Dr. Abbey Fernandez told me when she finally gave me the okay to return to work was to look around and appreciate my surroundings. In that way, you can really look at life from a whole new perspective. This really stuck to the back of my mind. Well, later that day, I received a phone call from Captain Flynn's office to report to his office on Friday morning at 9:00 sharp. At least this time, I was going to visit him with a clear view, and I knew what to expect could not wait until Friday. Finally, the big day arrived, so I got up extra early to make sure I was on time. As I got ready to visit the good Captain, I felt confident and relaxed and was looking forward to the visit. As I drove to the station, I could not wait to get started. I had a spring in my step. Finally, arriving and walking to the front door slowly, I opened the door. As usual, Sergeant Garcia gave me his familiar look and dropped his head. I just loudly wished him a good morning and started walking down the hall to the Captain's office. I really felt good. As I approached the office door, I stopped and knocked gently. As usual, the same loud voice invited me in, "Good morning, Dean." I returned the salutation. He waived me to sit down. "Well son, I received incredibly good reports from Dr. Abbey Fernandez, and as I told you before, then, and only then, would you be promoted to Detective. He calls out in his loud voice, "Mary come in here and bring Detective Dean's paperwork with you." Mary arrives in a matter of a few minutes, and as usual, she looks great. We exchanged glances, and she remarked, "Boy, Dean! The shrink helped you in more ways than you think. You look great!" Captain Flynn lifts his head and remarks, "If you two can stop with the compliments, maybe we can start here." "Sorry Captain," replies Mary. Captain Flynn clears his throat, "Dean, come over here and raise your right hand. Mary, you will serve as the witness." She replies that she would be happy to do so. He starts to read the proclamation and ends by reciting, "By the power given to me by the state of Florida, you are officially, as this date forward, addressed as Detective Dean." He sticks out his hand and congratulates me. Mary comes from around the desk, gives me a big hug, and does the same. Captain Flynn stops for a moment and looks at me and says, "Your father would have been proud of you." He caught me by surprise, and my only response was "Thank you, Captain." He handed me my gold shield, and I could not stop looking at it. Captain Flynn, in his loveable tone, says, "Ok detective, take the weekend off and start working on your project on Monday. Now get out of my office." As I looked around, Mary had already left the office, and as I opened the door and walked out, it really was a new beginning for me. Walking down the long corridor, it seemed getting to the front desk took longer, and as I reached Sergeant Garcia, he shouts out, "Good luck Detective Dean, and try not to fuck this up." I smiled, turned, thanked him, and replied, "I won't."

Dr. Abbey Fernandez constantly told me to look around my surroundings, to try and see something different, and to feel the area I am in. She said, "That way, it gives you a better view; stop the tunnel vision." I could not really understand what she was talking about, but that day, I decided to visit the Vizcaya Museum and Gardens. To a Floridian, a view of Vizcaya and its gardens feels like you are back in the northern providence of Spain. You feel like you are an explorer in a new and wonderful place in ancient times with all of its splendor and perpetuated myths, but instead of overlooking the Mediterranean Sea, it overlooks Biscayne Bay, a piece of Europe in Florida, a Miami project built by an American. It consists of history, innovation, nature, and beauty, with an international flavor of the past and presents a window into your own feelings and hopes. South Beach inspires the locals of many lands to realize what they can accomplish without hopelessness they left behind, memories of a warm climate, rhythmic music, a moment of illusion and grandeur, and the reality that it provides you with the opportunity, but it is up to you which road you take to achieve your goals. Thinking about a fresh start, Dean realizes that during his ceremony in Captain Flynn's office, Mary was really great, so he decided to give her a call and invite her out to lunch. He hesitates and thinks, "What if she turns me down?" What in hell do I have to lose? Nothing lost, nothing gained." He picks up the phone and calls. Mary's familiar voice answers, "Captain Flynn's office, how can I be of help to you?" "You can agree to go to lunch with me." Mary questions me, "Who is this?". "It's Detective Dean." "Hi Dean, how are you?" "Just great. Mary, I was just wondering if you would like to go to lunch with me?" She answers without hesitating, "Sure, next week sometime. Call me a day ahead of time. I am looking forward to it." She hangs up the phone. Dean was very pleasantly surprised. He takes a deep breath and remarks, "Boy, my life is changing. A beautiful woman like Mary did not hesitate to accept my lunch date, wow!" Reality quickly sets in as he realizes his work is just beginning. Well, let's start at the scene of the first fire, and the quickest way is to look at the fire reports. He realizes that he has to keep a low profile. As he starts to form a plan, he remembers that a neighbor down the street from his house is a lieutenant with the Miami Fire Department. As he begins his drive home, his mind is going a mile a minute. Finally, he pulls into the driveway and parks his car. He wants to make sure he approaches Frank, the neighbor, in a sincere way. He walks down the street to visit Frank. He knocks on the front door, and it quickly opens. Frank greets him, "Hey Dean, what's new? I haven't seen you in a long time." Dean answers, "You know the police department keeps you busy." "To what do I owe this visit, Dean?" "Well, Frank, I need a big favor. Do you know anyone down at the fire department headquarters who can get me some info about the warehouse fires and explosions without causing any suspicions?" "What is going on Dean?" Between us, Frank, I have been trying to find out what the cause is on my own. You know how hard promotions are today. The only way you are going to move up is to come up with something on your own time to even be considered. That's why it has to stay between us Frank or my ass is cooked." Frank looks at him with a puzzled look on his face. "I know what you mean, Dean." With his face still puzzled by the request, Frank tells Dean, "I have a friend who was just transferred to the records department because of a small transgression on his part, and I am sure he will help you; his name is Lieutenant Steve Blue. I will call him and explain the situation to him, and I will call you back." Thanks, Frank, I really appreciate it, and please keep this to yourself." "I will explain it to Steve. Believe me, he won't say a word." "Thanks again, Frank."

Mary is still on his mind, and he realizes it's been over two weeks since his last conversation with her. He decides to call her. As he nervously dials her cell phone, her familiar voice answers, and he is at a loss for words. Mary repeats, "Captain Flynn's office, can I help you?" Dean replies, "Mary, its Dean. How are you?" Her voice fills with excitement. "Dean! How is everything going with you?" "Things are okay, feeling good and making progress. Mary, how would you like to go out for lunch on Saturday?" She hesitates and answers, "Ok, but I love to sleep in late on Saturdays as it's my day off, so let's make it around one o'clock." Dean quickly agrees, "Ok, I will pick you up. What is your address?" As she explains where she lives, he nervously writes it down and sounds like a schoolboy on his first date. Mary remarks, "Boy, Dean, you sure have changed and are not anything like before. "Well, Mary, I have turned over a new leaf with your help," he chuckles, and says, "I look forward to Saturday." As he reaches his front door, he realizes that he promised himself that he would start to clean up his house. Today was the day to convert his museum into a home. He goes upstairs and changes his clothes into something more comfortable, runs down the steps, and, as he looks around, does not know where to begin. He goes into the garage, picks up two large trash cans, and puts them in the middle of the room. Then, he starts to just take down the pictures, plaques, and citations, and before he realizes, the living room and dining area are completely empty of the relics he lived with for all these years. He feels good as he starts to pull out the nails and fill the holes with a new beginning, not realizing its two o'clock in the morning and his date with Mary is fast approaching. He drops everything, runs upstairs, jumps in the shower, and quickly into bed. He sets his alarm, and as soon as his head hits the pillow, he is out cold. As the morning sun slowly creeps into his bedroom window, the sun shining in his rooms wakes him up. Slowly, he gets out of bed and runs downstairs to start breakfast. He realizes that he didn't brush his teeth. He runs back into the bathroom and starts to clean up. As he brushes his teeth, he starts to laugh, "I am acting like a teenager." He goes back downstairs and starts to make breakfast, remembering his new diet: cereal, toast, and coffee. It doesn't take him long to finish, and he quickly puts on his running shoes and shorts and unwillingly runs out the front door to try to run the two miles he set as his goal. This has been his routine for about three weeks, and he felt a sense of accomplishment today because he was able to run the entire two miles without stopping to walk. As he reaches his front door, he looks around for the first time to really look at his surroundings, something he never did before. He opens the front door, runs upstairs, throws his clothes on the bathroom floor, and jumps in the shower. The water feels great. He finally gets out, gets dressed, and walks down the steps. He looks at his watch and realizes it's about ten thirty in the morning. Slowly, he climbs the steps, walks into his bedroom, and starts to dress. He looks around for his cologne and splashes it on his face and neck. He looks at himself in the mirror and walks downstairs, out the front door, down the driveway, and into his car. As he starts the car and rolls down the driveway, he is mentally finding a way to Mary's house and realizes that her house is about an hour away, so he has plenty of time. He arrives at her house full of anxiety, walks up to the front door, and knocks. The front door opens, and Mary looks as beautiful as ever. She greets him with a big hello. "Dean, nice to see you. Come in." Mary quickly introduces him to her family and remarks, "Where are you taking me to lunch?" Dean remarks, "I thought we'd go to Miami Beach, take a walk down to Calle Ocho." Mary agrees, Ok, let's go going." They walk out the door. Dean opens the door for her, and Mary looks surprised. She does not say anything but has a smile on her face. The tension between them disappears as they lazily drive to their destination. Mary breaks the ice and comments, "You know, Dean, if someone would have suggested to me months ago to go out with you, I would have bet my life on it that it was not going to happen, but a lot has change for both of us, and now it feels right." "Thanks Mary, behind that beautiful woman lies a good heart," says Dean. She chuckles, "Shut up and drive!" They finally arrive at their destination but finding a parking spot seems almost impossible. Mary remarks, "Dean,

don't you have an official seal on your car? Just use it dummy."
"Why didn't I think of that?" Dean breaks out in a loud laugh
and just looks at her and smiles. As they walk down toward Calle
Ocho, they finally decide on a Cuban sandwich stand and order
a traditional sandwich. They both sit down on the sidewalk table,
just admiring the surroundings and the activity around them.
Their sandwiches arrive, and they both look at each other and
remark, "These monsters can feed the entire neighborhood, just
shut up and eat." The conversation and casual laughter made the
afternoon so pleasant that in his mind, he did not want it to end.
They talked so much that the monsters they ordered were gone.
Mary says, "I guess the neighbors are going to starve. This was a
great idea to stop here. It was delicious, thank you Dean." "I am
glad you enjoyed it, Mary. After this meal, we need to walk." As
they get up to start walking, Mary stumbles and Dean grabs her
hand. They both look at each other, continue to walk, and enjoy
each other's company. The afternoon just slips by. Mary looks at
her watch and remarks, "Dean, this afternoon will be extremely
hard to forget. Great food, great day, and terrific company, what
more can you ask for?" "Mary, the feeling is mutual. I hope this
will not be the last time we see each other." As the day starts to
come to an end, on the drive back to Mary's house, not too many
words were exchanged, but every so often they would look at each
other, and words could not replace what each glance felt like. As
he slowly arrives at the house, he stops and gets out to open, her
car door. Mary gets out and both walk to the front door. Dean
leans over and gently kisses her. It felt like they had known each
other all their lives. Mary looks at Dean, and words were not
necessary to describe the bond she felt with this screwball. As she
opens the door, she turns around and blows him a kiss. As Dean
slowly drives away, he realizes that this feeling was missing from
him for an awfully long time in his life.

CHAPTER 4

Driving home was bittersweet. He finally arrives home, gets out of his car, and smiles. As he gets closer to the front door, he hears the phone ringing. He hurriedly tries to open the door as fast as possible and finally picks up the phone. To his surprise, it's a familiar voice on the other end. It is his old partner, Officer Scott. "Hey Dean, how are you? Look let's just clear the air. We were partners for a long time. I was just totally pissed off at the time of our little predicament. Let's just forget it and move on." Dean replies, "You are right Scott, well, I forgot it five minutes after I left Captain Flynn's office." "Well, why didn't you call me you shit head?" Well, the long and short of it is that because of the situation, I had to go to a police doctor for me to stay on the job. Not too long ago, I was given the ok to return to work." "So, you are now an official screwball!" They both start laughing. "By the way, congrats on your promotion to Sergeant." "Thanks, it took me long enough. Right back at you Dean." "Thanks man." "Listen Dean, remember that crazy broad Grace Pastore, your old squeeze?" Dean chuckles, "Please don't remind me." "Well, a couple of days ago, we received a call about a disturbance at Performance Arts Studios. When we arrived, it was an all-out fistfight going on. We finally got everyone broken apart, and guess who is in the middle of the problem but good old Grace, with her face all bloodied up and screaming and talking shit. So, we call for a female officer to help us out. Dean, you should have been there. It turns out that your old friend Grace is now producing porn flicks. It was kind of funny, with about ten people fist fighting and screaming. It took us about twenty minutes just to break up this nude brawl. When you grabbed the people, you had no idea what you grabbed! Dean responds, "Are you kidding me?" Finally, we got things under control and cuffed everyone just to have some order. It was like a nude comedy movie, with everyone cuffed and naked. We looked at each other and just broke out laughing. We called the station for additional female officers to help us out. In all the years on the force, this was the craziest situation I have ever been involved in. It took us over an hour just to get everyone mirandized and clothed, and as we started to get to the bottom of the situation, the marijuana odor was just overwhelming. As we started to search each room and began checking all of their belongings, we started to find more and more pot all over the place along with cocaine, drug paraphernalia, and about four blocks of pot. It was a great pinch for the local good guys. So, we finally get the so-called performing cast of actors in the car, drive to the police station and run them through booking. All of us just start to laugh out loud like a bunch of nuts." "Well, Scott, thanks for the call. It was great to hear from you again. Next time don't wait so long, and let's get together for a beer." "Ok Dean, take care!"

As the phone call lingered on his thoughts, all kinds of scenarios flashed before him, and he felt that calling Captain Flynn would shed some light on other information for his current assignment. He picked up the phone and called the Captain's office. As usual, Mary answered the phone, and after normal chit chat ended, she told Dean not to forget to call her and then forwarded his call to Captain Flynn. He was nervously waiting to speak to his boss. Finally, the usual gruff voice picked up the phone and answered, "Well, Dean, how are you doing with our situation?" Dean, being prepared for him, remarks, "Captain, I don't know if you are aware of the drug pinch at Performing Arts Studios last Friday," and he proceeded to explain the pinch to him. Captain Flynn seemed lost in the comparison of the investigation and the drug bust, so Dean had to start thinking on his feet. Maybe there could be a possible lead into their own problem. Flynn remarked, "You are finally starting to think like a cop." "But Captain, the only problem in the case I am sure is going to be that it will be handled by the narcotics unit, and the only way I am going to get close to one of the suspects is Grace Pastore, if you can get me permission to talk down at the station without much explaining." "Well Dean, let me make a few phone calls, and I will get back to you. In the meantime, find out all of the info on your friend Grace." "Ok Captain, thank you." A few days later, Dean received a phone call from Captain Flynn, who goes on to explain, "Here is the situation. Mayor Alvarez is the kind of politician who is always looking out to cover his ass, so he has established a few committees with whom he meets quarterly, and they keep him informed of the situation in the community. One of them is called the Procedural Review Board. Its main focus is to make sure that for the Fire department investigations and procedures that go on in the Miami area, the Fire and Police departments don't violate the rights of either prisoners or detainees before they appear in court. The Mayor, after I had a lengthy conversation with him, has agreed to name you to his panel, giving you permission to ask and review previous cases on all detainees and incarcerated personnel without anyone getting suspicious of what you are looking for." "Oh my God, Captain! How in the hell did you pull that off?" "You dumb shit. Remember my original statement to you. The Mayor wants to get the heat off of his office, and what's better is that you get to investigate your case. Maybe now you realize the magnitude of the problem you are working on. Within a few weeks, your appointment will take place, and I will send you a special ID that you can show whenever you need to look up or request any info, either in the main computer or just walking in on any holding location to speak to any person or persons being held at any and all police stations in the Miami area." "Thank you, Captain. This gives me the time to put a plan together to try to get the handle on our situation." "Stay in touch with me." "Ok, Captain."

The next day, he gets out of bed slowly, walks to the bathroom, washes his face, and puts on his running gear. Still half asleep, he walks down the steps to the front door. He feels a sense of accomplishment, as, not too long ago, he would be gasping for air just to reach the front door. Now, he enjoys the daily two-mile run. The run clears his mind and gives him a new approach on the day. Quickly, the jog is over, and the case never seems that far away from his thoughts. He is trying to come up with an idea to see Grace without causing suspicion. He decides to call his old partner, Officer Scott, at the station. Finishing breakfast, he picks up the phone and calls the station. A familiar voice answered the phone. "Miami Metro front desk, how can I help you?" Good morning, Sergeant, this is Detective Dean." "How are you, and what can I do for you today?" "I would like to talk to Sergeant Scott." "Hold on and let me try to locate him for you. I am going to put you on hold for a minute." After a few minutes, Scott picks up the phone. "Dean, how are you man? You must have mental telepathy. I was going to call you. Your old flame Grace wants to talk to you, and I told her I would see what I could do, and here you are calling me." "Scott, that is the reason for the phone call, but I don't want to talk to her before I talk to you, and you fill me in on the situation she is in. Why don't we get together for lunch before I talk to her?" "Great, today is out of the question, but tomorrow will work out well for me." "Ok buddy, see you then at one o'clock at the 10th Street Café." Dean figured that since he was downtown, he might as well call Mary and take her to lunch. He gets in the car and dials her number. To his surprise, Captain Flynn answers the phone. "How are you, Captain? This is Detective Dean." "Detective Dean, how are you? I'm just fine, Dean. What can I do for you?"

"I would like to speak to Mary." "Any progress?" "As a matter of fact, Captain, I have a strong lead that might just help us open the case for us to stay on top of it." "That's great! Keep me informed." "Ok, Captain. Can you connect me with Mary?" "I will put you on hold and try to find her. I sent her downstairs to try to find your paperwork. It just arrived today, and I want to send it to you today, so do not hold her up." That is great, Captain." After a few minutes, Mary picks up the phone and says in her familiar voice, "Hi stranger, how are you?" "Just fine, Mary. I am downtown, and I thought I could take you to lunch." "Bad timing, Dean. The Captain has given me last minute reports that must be finished today, and I do not have time for lunch." "Mary, how about I pick up lunch for the both of us, and we can have lunch in your office, talk, and just be together?" "It is not an ideal situation for me," she ponders and finally accepts. "Ok, that is great! What do you want to eat?" "Whatever you choose is fine with me, Dean." "I will come by at 2 o'clock. That will give you time to get settled." "Ok Dean, see you then." As he figures out where to buy lunch for both of them, he finds a local café not too far from the police station. He looks in the phone book for their phone number and quickly calls and orders two Caesar salads with two large cokes to go. He waits a few minutes and slowly walks to the café to collect his orders. As he opens the door, the cashier is in front of him. He collects his order, pays the man, and starts to walk to the police station. As he opens the door, Sergeant Garcia greets him with a big smile on his face. "Good afternoon, Detective Dean, how are you this fine day?" To Dean's surprise, he responds, "Very well, thank you Sergeant." "Detective Dean, can you please come here for a moment before you go upstairs?" "Sure, what can I do for you?" "Nothing, just want to shake your hand." Dean has a surprised look on his face as he walks over and shakes the Sergeant's hand. "What is this all about, Sergeant?" "I just wanted to shake the hand of the luckiest man alive. I always knew there was a God above, and after I see you, I can truly believe it." He shakes his head in disbelief and chuckles. Dean is totally surprised as he walks to Mary's office. He finally arrives at her office with a surprised look on his face. He begins to explain to Mary what just happened, "What the hell is going on in this place, Mary? Everyone is treating me different." She smiles and answers him, "You dummy, they all know about your appointment to the Mayor's board." He smiles, "Oh well, let's eat lunch." "What is on the menu, asks Mary." "It is never dull around you," "The feeling is mutual, Mary." "Wow! My favorite chicken Caesar salad." Lunch flies by, and suddenly the office door opens, and Captain Flynn walks in and barks. "Is this my office or the lunchroom?" "Captain, detective Dean was kind enough to bring me lunch so I can finish all the work you need finished today." "Well, ok." As he walks back to his office, lunch is over, and they start to clean up all the trash as they look at each other and spontaneously embrace and kiss. They finally break apart; no words are needed to describe the moment. Dean walks out the door, takes only a few steps, and returns. He opens the door to stick his head in and smiles, "Thank you Mary, great lunch!" She smiles and sticks her tongue out at him. He starts to walk down the hallway. The door to the detective's rooms opens, and detective Gavin calls out, "Dean, if you have time, Lieutenant Chris would like to have a few words with you." "No problem." Lieutenant Ben is the man in charge of the department, a smallish man with a terrific reputation, a hands-on type of worker— no nonsense but easy to work with. "Come on in Dean," as he gets up from his desk, he extends his hand to him. This is the first time they have met each other. Lieutenant Ben seems truly sincere. "Well, Dean, it's our first meeting. We have been so busy around here. It is the first opportunity I got to meet you, and when detective Max told me you were in the building, I told him to make sure you stopped by to visit me so we could spend a little time talking." "Thank you, Lieutenant." "The scuttle in the whole building is that you are going to be named to the Mayor's board. Don't forget, if we can be any help to you, do not hesitate to call me." "Thank you, Lieutenant. I really appreciate all the help I can get." "Thanks again and have a good day detective." As he walks out the door, he thinks to himself, "Not too long ago, all I remembered was jeers and verbal abuse, but when you think about it, I really deserved it. It is nice to talk to everyone on an equal basis. Who in the hell am I fooling? The only reason they even bothered to say hello is because of my pending appointment to the Mayor's board. Ha-ha! Revenge is best served cold. This has been a very productive day. Why not continue?" He decides to visit the fire department office and check on his contact at the record department. "Let me check my notes and see who the contact person was. I can't remember the guy's name." As he starts to leaf through the notes, he finds that the contact person's name is Officer Parker. As he slowly starts to walk through the police station door, he starts to feel good about himself and starts to snicker about what just happened to him. He walks down the street to his car and remarks to himself, "I knew it was too good to last." There is a parking ticket on his windshield. "Well, maybe this newfound good fortune can get this ticket fixed. The Miami fire department is located twenty-five minutes away. Thank goodness for GPS!" He finally arrives, and no different from any other government building, it is the biggest on the block. The problem is just finding a parking space. This time, he makes sure to place his official plaque on the dashboard to avoid another surprise. As I approach the building and step through the front door, my only concern is to find out where the record department is located, so I take a quick at the location marquee, which is located in room 410. Walking to the elevator, in my own mind, I am trying to figure out how to handle this situation: Do I use my newfound position or just follow the nice guy approach? As I reach the door and walk in, all I see is a very large space that looks like a record file warehouse. No color, and very poorly lit with a very large counter and a small bell next to a sign that reads "Service, ring twice." As I bang hard on the bell, a very attractive young woman approaches the counter with a smile. "Good afternoon. How can I be of help to you?" In my mind, I had other ideas, but quickly, my thoughts came back to reality. We both smiled at each other, and I explained to her who I was and that I would really appreciate her help. She smiled, "First, let's see some identification." "I quickly showed her my ID, and she asked me what I needed." Still a little confused, I explained to her that I was investigating a homicide in the waterfront area, read about the sudden fires in the same area, and figured it would be a good place to start. She explained that it would really help if I could give her a date to start the search on her computer. "Just let me look at my notes." As I started to leaf through my note pad, I was conscious not to give her too much info, so I gave her the date of the first fire. I figured the circumstances in all the fires were very similar, so it would not really matter which date I give her. She took the info and told me to hang on while she tracks it on the computer. "In the meantime, sit down and relax for a few minutes." It was kind of hard to sit. No chairs around, so I just leaned on the counter and looked around. She disappeared from view, returned about ten minutes later, and explained to me that those files were not available at this time, and the only way I could see them was to talk to her supervisor, Officer Parker. I acted surprised, but that was my connection at the fire department. "By the way, what is your name?" "Tracy," she answered. "Could you do me a favor and see if I can talk to Officer Parker?" "Ok, let me call him and ask if it's at all possible for you to stop by and talk to him." She walked into the next room and quickly told me to go to room

420. "Officer Parker will be waiting for you." I thanked her for her help and walked down the hall to his office. As I approached the door, I took a deep breath, not to look too anxious, and knocked on the door. A voice told me to come in. As I opened the door, I was greeted by Officer Parker. We both exchanged pleasantries, and he asked me to sit down. I explained to Officer Parker what I needed. He responded by stating that he doesn't see a problem and will call Tracy to authorize the information I needed. "And tell her to just sign my name on the file. If it is helpful, tell her to make a copy, and anything else that can help you. Maybe down the road, you can help me out with a problem." "Dean replies, "Anytime," and hands him his business card. "Just give me a few minutes to call Tracy and give her the ok." Dean thanks him again and waits for a few minutes while he makes the phone call. "Ok Dean, give her a few minutes. I told her to set you up in a separate area so you can take your time." He gets up, shakes his hand, and slowly walks out the door. As he walks back to the warehouse, he opens the door and Tracy greets him, "Follow me, and I will set you up in a private room. I will bring you the files requested." Dean thanks her and takes his jacket off. No sooner is his jacket off, Tracy walks in with the files and drops them on his desk. "Well, that is all the info pertaining to the fire, detective." "Thank you for all your help, Tracy." She smiles and walks away. Dean did not realize the mounds of reports, photos, and general information involved in a fire department investigation. Two folders just with photos, diagrams, maps, a complete layout of the building, and fire damage patterns. Another folder contained tests on the flammability properties and flame-spreading pattern of materials. There was so much info that he started getting a headache. As he slowly reads the material in front of him, he is looking for a needle in a haystack. He stops, takes a few minutes, and starts to think that there has to be a clue about what and how this fire started. Finally, he

stumbles on the most important assumption: Which type of material was found at the scene of the fire and which kind of heat produced the intensity to make the building fall and crumble. The report goes on to explain that the cause of the fire was ashes from shipping crates with a residue of straw and a heavy pungent odor. Their final belief was that the fire and explosion were caused by anhydrous ammonia. Dean realizes he must do some research, and the accurate way is to get to the computer as soon as possible. He rushes to get home with his mind running a mile a minute. For the first time, he is really excited about his work, a feeling he has not felt for a very long time. Home at last, he walks over to the computer and begins his research. Nothing seemed fast enough for him, and the excitement had taken over. He finally realizes that he needs to slow down, take a deep breath, and get back to normalcy. "Wow, what a rush!" The fire department reports speak of anhydrous ammonia. He quickly finds the subject matter, and it reads just like the report: combustion, explosive gives out a pungent odor, the irritant property of ammonia, toxic gases, and fire hazards. He realizes that he is on the right track. Curiosity is making him forget that his big day is quickly approaching, and the only way to settle his nerves is to try and take his mind off his work, so he settles for a quick meal and starts to try to complete his home project. He starts to paint the living room, but it is of no use. He is only kidding himself; he can't get the case off his mind. After painfully completing the dining and living rooms, morning cannot come soon enough. He heads upstairs to pick out what he is going to wear, sets his alarm for six o'clock, and dives into bed. Quickly, it is lights out, and it seems like no time at all as the alarm clock is ringing, and it is time to get up. As he slowly opens his eyes, jumps out of bed, and walks to the bathroom, he jumps in the shower and moves out as quickly as possible. He gets dressed, walks downstairs, and out the front door, off to Captain Flynn's office. As he approaches the police station, he feels that he finally belongs. He quickly parks his car down the street, gets to the front door, and, as usual, Sergeant Garcia greets him with a big smile and a thumbs up. He looks over and just smiles. He continues down the hall to the Captain's office, knocks, and walks in. A surprised Mary looks up and remarks, "Boy, Dean! You really got here early. Do you have time for a cup of coffee?" "Thanks, Mary. I sure can use one black, no sugar. Well, the coffee pot is just around the corner, and while you're at it, bring me one cream two sugars." "No problem." Soon, they start to enjoy their coffee. Captain Flynn walks in and seems truly surprised to see Detective Dean waiting. He grunts as usual and barks out, "Give me five minutes to have my coffee, and then we can complete the paperwork and games." "There are no games with me Mary, I can promise you." "Ok, I will talk to you later. I have to get back to work. You really know how to screw up a girl's good day Dean." Driving to the fire department headquarters, Dean was trying to set some sort of game plan to try and make his day a little productive. He finally arrives at his destination, walks in the front door, and quickly takes the elevator to the fourth floor. He walks down the hall, opens the door, and notices on the counter a note from Tracy explaining to him that all the information she could find is on the desk in the next room. She was sorry that she missed him, but she had to leave to take care of a family matter this morning. He walks around the corner to the area he used before, and on the desk are a number of files. He thinks to himself, "Time to get to work." He takes his jacket off and starts to read. Investigation photos of the areas, diagrams of the building, fire damage patterns, and flammability patterns of the previous fire did not lead to a conclusive cause. The first one was different because a body was found in the ashes. The ones between the first and the last case didn't offer any clues, no set pattern. The last one was the only one with a specific conclusion. It seemed to him that, in the first one, there was an attempt to cover the body and get rid of the evidence. The ones after it were just to throw the fire investigators off track. In the last one, the fire ignited too quickly. It was too sloppy a job, but they all seemed to have very similar patterns. A person ignited the torch. The only thing that could be concluded is that Dean had developed a very large migraine. He gathered all the files and dropped them off at the front counter. Finally, he reaches the first floor and out the door; the fresh air seems to rejuvenate his mind. He thinks to himself, "Well, another day's work ends in total futility." He finally gets home up the stairs to his bedroom, flops in his bed, mentally exhausted, and is eventually out like a light.

"I need to get back to the fire department headquarters and continue to further check the other fires to see if there is a connection." Dean reaches for his cell phone, searches for Tracy's number, and dials. Within a very few rings, the phone is answered. What a surprise! "Miami fire department headquarters, how can I help you?" "Would you please connect me to extension 622? Thank you." A familiar voice on the other end answers, "Good afternoon, how can I help you?" "Hi Tracy, Detective Dean here. Would it be possible to stop over tomorrow? I need to check on the remaining fires." "I can be of help, Dean, if you give me the date of the file, I pulled out for you. I will just extract all the fires reported around the six-month period. That will give you a good idea timewise." "That would be great, Tracy." "I will have that for you Dean." "See you tomorrow, and thanks again." It seems that sooner or later, he starts to think about Mary, so he decides to give her a call. "Captain Flynn's office, how can I help you?" "Hello, Mary. It's Dean." "You must have telepathy! I was just about to call you and thank you for the flowers and the wonderful evening." "The feeling is mutual. Soon you and I will have to sit down and have a long talk." "Why so serious, Dean?" "Mary, I just don't want to lose you." Complete silence takes over. "Mary, are you still there?" "I am still here, Dean." "What happened?" "You just took me by surprise. I did not expect that from you." "Don't you realize that you helped me change and get my life on track? I just want to make sure we stay on the same track together." "Now you listen, Dean, you better not be playing."

CHAPTER 5

As many times I delivered prisoners to the detention center, today it seems completely different. Perhaps it's the idea that I am no longer in uniform and being treated along with the masses. Today, as I walked in the door and showed my ID, it felt like a good new dimension of respect. Everyone was very polite—a strange feeling. As I approached the front desk, the officer asked me to secure my weapon and register. He promptly took me to Sergeant Lisa's office, and she greeted me. Very candid and to the point, "How can I help you detective?" I said, "I need to speak to Grace Pastore." She acted a little confused and asked, "Any particular reason for visiting Ms. Pastore?" "I will explain it to you out of courtesy to a fellow officer. You may or not know that I serve on the Mayor's board, and part of the Mayor's agenda is to make sure all persons, no matter what gender or color, are treated with decency and respect during and while under the protection of the city. For your information, Sergeant, I happened to pick out Ms. Pastore because of the humorous circumstances of her arrest, which was handled by my old partner Sergeant Scott." "Sorry Detective, I meant no disrespect. It was just my curiosity. I will have her taken to interview room number ten." "Thank you, Sergeant. "Detective Dean, I will get you her arrest paperwork as well." Damn, that felt good. As I slowly walked to the interview room, I realized that I have to be careful of all my actions to keep everyone involved off their guard about my real intentions. Within ten minutes, Officer Elana escorts Grace to the room. I was surprised at how different she looked since the last time I was in her company. She looked older and slimmer, with a lost look in her eyes. As our eyes met, her face lit up, and a very big smile appeared. The officer asked if I wanted her to stay in the room, and I asked her to wait outside the door. No sooner she walked out the door, Grace made sure she was out of the room, and with her handcuffed hands gave me a quick embrace and sat down. I could see her eyes tearing up. I hesitated for a moment and broke the ice. "Grace, Sergeant Scott told me that you had some very important information that could help me. Let's get ground rules out in the open. Grace, I will help you as much as possible, but the first time you try to con me, it's all over, do you understand me?" Without hesitation, she answers, "I do understand you loud and clear Dean." "Grace, are you aware of the charges you are facing? Let me read them to you so there is no misunderstanding: possession of various drug paraphernalia, possession of one kilo of marijuana, ten grams of cocaine, and other substances..." She interrupts me, "But Dean there were other people involved." "I realize that Grace, but it all took place in your studios." She slumps her head down and becomes very quiet. "Grace, you are possibly facing a very long sentence, thousands of dollars in fines, and a minimum jail sentence of fifteen years. Let's be honest with each other Grace." "I know Dean. I am in a risky business, and the people I deal with drugs are very dangerous." "Well Grace, if you want to help yourself, think about the situation you're in and make sure that when I come back, you are not wasting my time. Let me tell you, think about our conversation. I will be back next week." "Ok Dean, thank you."

As he gets up and knocks on the door, Officer Elana walks in, motions to Grace to get up. She turns around and nods her head at Dean. He waits a few minutes until they disappear down the hall. He walks out of the room and reaches the front desk area, where he is greeted by Sergeant Lisa. "Have a good day, Detective." "Thank you, Sergeant Lisa." No sooner does he get out of the front door; his cell phone starts to ring. He glances at the number, and it's not familiar to him so he ignores it. "If it's important they will leave a message," he thinks to himself. He climbs into his car, puts on his seatbelt, and the missed call is starting to bother him, so he unbuckles the belt. To his surprise, it is Lieutenant Ben, Chief of Detectives. "I wonder what he wants." Dean calls the number, and after a few rings, Lieutenant Ben answers the phone, "Lieutenant Ben here, how can I help you?" "Detective Dean returning your call. What can I do for you Lieutenant?" "I just received a call from the detention center informing me that you visited Grace Pastore. Any specific reason for the visit?" "Lieutenant, the news travels fast!" "You know how things are, Detective." "I am sure Sergeant Lisa filled you in but let me explain it to you like I did Sergeant Lisa; I represent the Mayor. You are familiar with the Mayor and his various pet projects. Well, after the situation, I am here to make sure that under his administration, we have little or no police brutality charges filed against this administration, and I am sure you are aware that Ms. Pastore's case made all the local media stations. My job is to make sure that everything and everyone follows the letter of the law to its fullest. So, before you, the police department, and the Mayor get served with a lawsuit, I must check the whole arrest procedure." "That seems a little strange to me detective." "Well, Lieutenant, I really don't think the Mayor cares about your opinion; he just wants to make sure his ass is covered, and let's be real about it, it seems a little possible under the circumstances of the arrest. Let me explain the facts to you, Lieutenant. It took ten uniformed officers to round up eight nude persons running around the building and further, and after they were finally controlled, numerous drugs, etc., were found all over the studio. Let me refresh your memory of what the news called it: the new version of the Miami keystone cops." "I can see your point detective." "I am glad we are both on the same page, Lieutenant. Have a good day." While driving home, he realizes how much his life has changed, so he decides to take a few days off and finish his home project once and for all. It has been taking too long. Then, he would spend quality time with Mary. He finally arrives at his house, calls Mary, and the conversation lasts for over twenty minutes. He invites her over for dinner. He sits down on the couch for a few minutes, and before you know it, he falls sound asleep. He wakes up, not realizing that he spent the night on the couch, goes upstairs, washes up, and decides to go for a quick jog. Out the door, and his two-mile jog seems to fly by. To his surprise, no aches or pain. He thinks to himself, "It seems like I am getting in better shape." He goes upstairs and takes a shower, makes breakfast for himself, and starts to try to complete his renovation project. The days seem to fly quickly by, and to his surprise, the work is finally completed. Finally, it's all over. He looks around and feels he has done a good job. The place looks great, nice, and clean. He remembers what the house looked like before. He finishes cleaning up and starts to get ready for his date with Mary. The weekend just flew by, and he feels relieved, refreshed, and ready for another day of work. He gets in his car and finally arrives at his destination, the Miami Detention Center. A little apprehensive of what Grace has in store for him, he walks up to the front desk and is greeted by Sergeant Lisa, who says, "Back again, Detective?" "Just part of the job, Sergeant, you know the routine." "Detective, check your firearm and sign the book, and I will call over for your prisoner. Thank you, Detective, use room ten again." As he sits waiting for Grace, his mind wanders from subject to subject about what to ask her. Finally, she gets into the room, and the guard waits outside. Grace greets him with a big smile. "Good morning, Dean, how are you?" "Just fine, Grace." "Dean, I don't know where to start." "Just tell me how you got involved." "Dean, as you already know, four years ago, I was involved with a group of people in the local drug trade. We got caught, were taken to trial, and were sentenced. I took most of the brunt of the charges, kept my mouth shut, and did my time. After my release, I was again approached by the same people I had been involved with before. I really did not want to get involved with them again, but you know how it is, Dean. Just out of jail, no money, no place to stay. I was totally lost, so I decided to listen to their offer. A few weeks later, I was approached again. They told me they would set me up in a business they knew that I was involved with—the porn film business—in a very limited way, and that is how Performing Arts Studios started. How in hell was I going to turn this opportunity down? Within a few weeks, I had a building, all the equipment, and the staff needed to start production. They even supplied scripts. It was great. I did my thing and was given a salary of five hundred dollars a week. I knew this gravy train had a hidden agenda, but for the meantime, I just enjoyed it, and things got even better when I met you at the Bolero Bar. We struck up a nice working relationship. You gave me the comfort that I had a Miami cop hanging around the studio, and when my partner found out about our relationship, they were pissed off. But soon, they realized that it gave the studio some legitimacy. Dean, admit it, we had a good time while it lasted." Dean just smiles at Grace reluctantly, "Go on." I was upstairs, and one late night I was awaken by some noise from downstairs. Quietly, I walked down to take a look, and the storage room door was open. It was strange, because it had a very huge lock on it. I walked in the room, and to my surprise, Cooper Hunter, my benefactor, was opening some small crate, and I caught him off guard. As he turned around, he got startled and started to scream at me, "God damn it, Grace, don't you ever come in this room, Do you understand me?" I tried to reason with him, and he just told me to get the fuck out of the room." Dean asked, "What does he look like?" "About 6' 2", well-tanned, very muscular; he spends time at the gym. After that commotion, I just walked back upstairs to my room, but my curiosity got the better of me, so I started to notice all the activities that took place." "Grace, tell me how you know this guy?" "At one time, he was a big-time pimp in the downtown area. He had all the girls, and when I was released from jail, I met him downtown. He told me he would take care of me, but I told him to get lost as it wasn't my thing. I was not going to become one of his whores. He just smiled and repeated it again, "I will be talking to you, Grace." I just ignored him and went about my business; would you believe he was the guy that set me up with the studio." "What else do you know about him?" "Besides running all the girls, he was connected to a very large drug family. The story around town was that he had plenty of cash and drugs at his disposal. Weeks went by after the incident, and I began to notice that almost every two weeks, we receive a shipment of small crates. Cooper would always be present for the deliveries. I really started to get curious." "Grace, hold on. Did you ever even get a look at what was in those crates?" "It was kind of strange. It looked like rolls of wallpaper, but not the regular types." "What do you mean?" "These rolls looked like cloth that is used to paint pictures. I realized there was something going on, and I was going to find out what it was." "So, what happened?" "As you well know, Dean, the last time I did some time, my roommate was in for burglary, and she taught me how to pick locks, so the first opportunity I got, I strolled downstairs late at night and picked the lock open. To my surprise, there were just a few empty crates. The only thing that caught my eye was the markings on the side of the crates stamped GI IMPORTING CO. PANAMA CITY, PANAMA, and a milky substance on the floor that looked like Lisa Sugar. I wondered what the secrecy was all about." Dean breaks out in a loud laugh. "What is so funny, Dean?" "Grace, you are a woman with many hidden talents." "Dean, I have a few more, but my hands are cuffed." He looks at her and remarks, "So far, Grace, all you have told me is bullshit. I told you, Grace, if you try to con me, I will walk away and never come back." "No Dean, I have something special, ok?" "Let's get on with it." She reaches over, takes a drink of water, and starts to tell Dean that a week later, she decided to go out and have a few drinks at the Bolero Bar. So, after getting a load on, she headed home. When she opened the front door, she noticed that one of the studio lights was on. "Dean, you remember the room that we used for all of our film work. The one that looks like an apartment? I figured I must have left it on, and to my surprise, when I walked in, there on the couch was a beautiful young woman who was passed out. I raised my voice to get her attention, and she woke up. I asked her, 'What are you doing here? This is private property.' She slowly looks up, and I can tell that this girl is stoned. She said, 'Don't worry, I am Cooper's girlfriend.' I felt sorry for her. She started crying and told me, 'That son of a bitch just walked out on me, just left me here, and told me to get lost. Fuck him. I am not getting lost.' She sits up, grabs her handbag, and pulls out a bag of coke. She looks at me with her droopy eyes and asks if I want to join her. I said, 'No., thanks.' Then, she says, 'Well, I might as well snort a few more lines. Give me a moment. I have a bottle of wine. We can drink wine. It is always good with coke,' she giggles. I return quickly, and the two of us just talk about everything under the sun. We had a good time just talking. After all this time, I don't even know her name. She tells me that her name is Paige Green." Dean's face turns completely white. "Grace, what was her name again?" "Paige Green." Grace remarks, "Dean, are you ok? Your face is as white as a ghost." He takes a deep breath and tells Grace, "I am fine just getting over a bad stomach virus and still not fully recovered." Dean's head is filled with mixed emotions. Grace notices he is still not fully responding to her, so she reaches over and gives him a bottle of water. "Take a drink, Dean, and you will feel better." Slowly, he takes the cap off, takes a good, long drink, and tries to get his composure back.

"Give me a few minutes, Grace." She realizes he is not feeling well and asks, "Do you want me to call the guard?" He motions, asking for a few more minutes. He tries to act like himself again and asks what else she told Grace. This time, Grace gets very quiet and tells Dean to get close to her. "Why all the hush, Grace?" "Paige was pretty wasted. She leaned over to me and almost fell on her face. I sat her back up on the couch." She says to me, 'Grace, I have a secret, and I have to tell someone before I kill myself.' With all of my drug use, I thought she was just another wasted strung-out bitch telling me a tale of lies. I said to her, 'Ok Paige, you can tell me. I can keep a secret.' She tells me that she is the DEA agent working undercover on a case. I just started laughing, and the more I laughed, the madder she became. Finally, both of us fell asleep, and when I woke up in the morning, she was gone. The next day, late in the afternoon, Cooper comes to the studio. Usually, he just walks around and leaves without saying hello to me, but on this day, he made it a point to come over and start a conversation and asked me how things were going. Then, he casually asked me, 'When you came in last night, was there anyone in the studio?' I said, 'Oh yes, I met your girlfriend, Paige. Wow, Cooper! Is she always that strung out?' 'Well, Grace, she has a habit. She is beautiful, but that beauty is not going to last long hitting the drugs.' 'Well, I guess you can always trade her in for a new model.' He gave me a look like he wanted to kill me. I just kept my mouth shut and started to walk away. Then he says to me, 'By the way Grace, what did you guys talk about? 'Last night? Just some girl talk, but nothing really.' 'Grace, explain what you mean by nothing.' 'Both of us got very drunk, and she told me a secret that she was an undercover DEA agent. I just started to laugh, and she became very angry with me. Cooper, she was just wasted.' He looked at me with these cobra eyes." Dean says, "Grace, what in the hell are cobra eyes?" "Dean, haven't you watched hunting channels on TV? When they show a cobra ready to strike at his prey? Their eyes get really black. Well, that's the way Cooper's eyes looked. He hesitated for a minute, reached in his pocket, pulled out a roll of hundred-dollar bills, and gave me four of them. I grabbed the money and thanked him. Then he said, 'That's one thing Grace. You know how to keep your mouth shut.' I just responded, 'You can always count on me Cooper." The matter was closed as far as I was concerned, but about four weeks later, an explosion and fire were reported on the local news, stating that a body was found, and the remains were confirmed to be of Paige Green. Then, I realized that I had Cooper by the short hairs. I just had to keep my mouth shut and use the information later." Dean says, "Grace, listen to me. Now, I am going to explain it to you just once; under no circumstances are you to repeat what you just told me to anyone, and I mean no one. Do you understand what I just told you?" "Yes Dean, I understand." "If you are asked why I visited you on two occasions, you just tell them we were talking about the night of your arrest. I just wanted to make sure that all parties involved were treated well." Grace looked puzzled, "Ok Dean, whatever you say. Can you do anything to help me Dean?" "Grace, just make sure you remember what I just told you and leave it to me. I am going to help you." Grace's face lit up. "I will be in touch." He got up and knocked on the door. The officer motioned Grace to get up; this time, she seemed to have more enthusiasm as she walked out of the room. Dean just sat there for a few minutes and realized that he could finally solve this case. He gets up, quickly checks out, and walks out the door. As he sits in his car, it finally hits him. He has concrete evidence, names, locations, and motive, and that's only the beginning. He needs a plan to arrive at the conclusion, and most importantly, he has the resources to do that. His head is still spinning with anxiety and enthusiasm. He takes a deep breath and tries to calm down. He picks up his cell phone and calls Captain Flynn's office. The phone is answered not fast enough for him, but a familiar voice says, "Captain Flynn's office, Mary speaking. Dean! How are you feeling?" "Good, sweetheart, is the boss in?" "Yes." "Would you ask him if he has the time to meet me today? It is very important." "Ok, hold on." In a few minutes, Mary gets back on the phone and tells Dean that the Captain can see him in one hour. "Ok Mary, thank you. See you then." Dean hangs up and thinks to himself, "I have to keep my composure, explain the complete situation to the Captain and come up with a plan to best take advantage of our opportunity. My head is still spinning from the interview with Grace. As I try to clear my head, the half-hour ride to Captain Flynn's office is really going to help me. I feel like a rookie making his first arrest, but this is an opportunity to prove to myself that I belong. I take my time driving to the police station, and as I turn down the street, as usual, parking is the biggest problem. But ahead, a parking space quickly opens. I drive in, flip down my parking badge, and start to walk down the street. I get to the door and, as usual, I am greeted by Sergeant Garcia's smiling face. "Good morning, Detective Dean, how are you today?" "Fine, thank you, Sergeant." I take my time walking to the Captain's office and quietly open the door. Mary's big smile greets me. I lean over and give her a kiss. "Hello Dean, let me check with the Captain if he is ready for you." She returns in a few minutes and tells me to go in. "Morning Dean, Mary tells me that you had something very important that you wanted to speak to me about; please sit down." As I go through the interview with him explaining all the details, he tells me how pleased he is with the progress, "You did a great job." He takes a deep breath and asks my opinion on whether I felt we should move forward, a sign of confidence. First, Captain, you should apprise Mayor Alvarez of the situation we are facing, and secondly, we should keep this in-house. Let's not involve Lieutenant Ben and the department for the time being." "Do you think it is a good idea?" "Look at it this way. I technically work for you and the Mayor. If we get anyone else involved at this point, it can screw up the element of surprise." He thinks for a minute and says, "I think you are right." "Captain, your help combined with the Mayor's influence is the only way the DEA is going to sit down and talk about the problem we both face. They really don't want to air out old laundry with anyone outside of their department. With the Mayor involved, they will not just shove it under the rug." "You have a point, Dean. The Mayor can promise them that this matter will be a need-to-know situation." "What do you mean me and the Mayor? When we meet, you will be part of the discussion and will contact the Mayor's office for an appointment to start formulating a plan that we can present. I will be in touch." As I get up and close the door behind me, his loud voice comes over the intercom. "Mary, get me the Mayor's office on the phone." "Ok, Captain." Mary waves to me to hold on as she dials the phone. In a very short time, the phone is answered, "Mayor's office, how can I help you?" "This is Captain Flynn's office. Could you please connect me with the Mayor's secretary?" "Hold on please." "Mayor Alvarez's office, Dana speaking. How can I help you?" "Hi, Dana, it is Mary from Captain Flynn's office." "How are you, Dana?" "You know how it is, more work than I can handle." "I know the feeling." "Listen, Dana, my boss needs to speak to the Mayor." "Hold on, I will connect you." "Captain Flynn, pick up line two; the Mayor will be on in a few minutes." As Flynn anxiously awaits, the Mayor answers, "Captain, how are you, and how is our project coming along?" "That is why I am calling your honor." The detective we assigned to the case has very good news, and both of us would like to discuss the situation with you." "Captain, hold on a minute. While I have Dana, let me check my calendar." "Thank you, your honor." A few minutes go by, and the Mayor gets back on the phone. "Captain, bring him to my office tomorrow at 9:00." "Thank you, your honor, we will see you tomorrow." He hangs up quickly and, as usual, screams out to Mary to get a hold of Detective Dean. "Captain, he is still here." "Great! Send him in my office." "Dean, you heard him. Go in." Dean knocks on the door and walks in. "Dean, tomorrow at 9:00 am, we have a meeting with the Mayor. Pick me up here at 8:00 sharp, and we will go together. That's all and don't be late." Dean says, "Thank you, Captain," and walks out the door. Mary looks at him and asks, "What's up Dean?" He replies, "I have to meet the Mayor tomorrow." She has a worried look on her face. "Don't worry Mary, I am not in trouble." "You better not be." "I will call you later." As he walks down the hallway and out the door, he bumps into his old partner, Sergeant Scott. "Hello, superstar! How is everything going?" "Great." He takes Scott aside and says, "Listen Scotty. I may be able to get you out of uniform. Can I count on you?" "Dean, do you really have to ask that question, you jerk? What's up?" "Just hang in there, and I will be in touch. It's only between us. Do you understand me?" "No problem, Dean. I will wait for your call." He drives home, and for once, he doesn't have any projects. It's an easy night to get ready for tomorrow morning. The morning comes too soon, and once again, on his drive to the office today, he feels confident and ready for the challenge ahead. He arrives at the police station and walks in. To his surprise, no Sergeant Garcia. He continues down the hall, approaches his destination, knocks, and walks in. "Good morning, Mary." "Good morning, Dean. The boss is waiting for you. I will tell him that you are here. Captain, Detective Dean is here." "I will be right out. By the way, Dean, you look great! New suit?" "As a matter of fact, yes. I broke down and spent some money." "Looks great." "Thank you!" "Ok Dean let's go. Dean, I will drive." "Ok, Captain. As they walk to the door, a smiley Garcia greets them, "Good morning gentlemen." "Good morning, Sergeant." Rank has its privileges; the Captain's car is parked in the front row. They both get in, and after only 20 minutes, they arrive at City Hall, park up front, and start to walk in. As they approach the Mayor's office, Dean opens the door, and Dana, the Mayor's secretary, is waiting for them. She escorts them to the Mayor's office, knocks on the door, sticks her head in, and tells the Mayor that his visitors have arrived. "Gentlemen, can I get you some coffee?" "Yes, thank you. One black and one sugar." The Mayor extends his hand and greets both of them, "Please sit down. Dana will be back in a minute with the coffee. Let's wait for her so that we will not be interrupted." As they settle in their seats, Dana walks in and distributes their morning coffee. The Mayor instructs her, "No disruptions." "Yes sir." "Ok, gents, tell me the news." Captain Flynn introduces Detective Dean to the Mayor and explains to him that he is responsible for the investigation, so it is best if he brings him up to date. Dean clears his throat and explains his complete interview with Grace Pastore. The Mayor is amazed at the information and the potential that has been presented to him. Dean finishes, and the Mayor remarks, "You picked the right person for the job." "Thank you, sir." The Mayor takes a sip of his coffee and is still trying to evaluate all the information. He then asks, "How should we proceed?" Dean interrupts, "May I, Captain? "Sure, go-ahead Dean." "Your honor, as I explained to the Captain, I feel that this matter, for the time being, should be kept in house to minimize a possible leak." "You are right, Dean, but the first problem we face is to be able to find out how much information Agent Paige gave to the local DEA office or to her boss." "That is where we need your political influence and power." The Mayor smiles, "I think I can arrange that." The next situation, your honor, is that Grace Pastore's bail hearing is coming up in two weeks. We need you to talk to the DA to make sure she gets a normal bail so that we can get her back on the street, making it possible for her boss, Cooper Hunter, to be able to help with the bail without raising suspicion. Then, I can speak with Grace Pastore and explain to her the situation as well as how important her further cooperation is in this case." "Dean, you are making a very good point. Do you require additional help in this matter?" "At this time, your honor, I would like to talk to the Captain and draw on his experience in this matter." "Well gents, let me tell you that you have made my day, and I will start to work on the matter quickly. I will be in touch with Captain Flynn about my progress. Again, Captain Flynn and Detective Dean, a very well thought out approach." "Thank you, Mayor, have a great day!" They both get up and slowly walk out of his office. "Dean, a very professional presentation and well done." "Thank you, Captain." Explain to me the additional help. This is where I need your clout and experience, Captain. We both know that this case can only go forward with the help of Grace Pastore, but we have to use her so that she feels she is in control. Therefore, we need to keep a very close eye on her without her knowledge, and the only person that I trust is my old partner, Sergeant Scott. He knows the downtown area and all the players." "You gave me the impression earlier that you guys did not get along." "We have been going back and forth since the days at the academy, but he is my closest friend, like a brother, and has always been there for me. He was the person who put me on to Grace Pastore." "Well, Dean, let's get all the pieces in place before we bring him in." "Ok, Captain."

"Mary, call Dean." "Ok, Captain." Usually, Dean takes his time answering his phone, but to Mary's surprise, after only a few rings, he answers, "Hello, Mary." "Dean, Captain Flynn wants to speak to you. Hold on, and I will transfer you." "Good afternoon, Dean, the Mayor called me about an hour ago and wants us to meet him on Friday morning at the Main Marina at 6:30 am sharp. We are going on a fishing trip." Dean responds, "Wow, I hate fishing." "Ok Captain, do you want me to pick you up?" "No, I will meet you there, and don't be late." "Captain, can you get Mary back on the phone?" Mary comes on the phone, "Dean, what's up?" "Mary, if you are available on Saturday night, I would love to cook dinner for you at my house." "Dean, that would be great, what time?" "How about 6:30?" "Ok, see you on Saturday."

As he gets off the phone, he realizes he should start to map out a plan so that all parties can get on board. So, he decides to go home and just concentrate on his ideas. He is slowly realizing that it takes more to be a detective than just arresting people. He is really starting to enjoy his job and the preparation it takes to make it work. The day quickly passes, and the anxiety of the next day's task gets him thinking. It seems that, as soon as he closes his eyes, it is time to get up. He grabs a quick cup of coffee and is off to downtown Miami. The roads are clear, and it seems like a ghost town, a pleasant drive. He reaches his destination, and as he gets out of his car, he hears a familiar voice calling, "Good morning, Dean." "Good morning, Captain." "How are you, ready?" "I sure am Captain. Let's get it over with, as I really don't like fishing either." "That is definitely one thing we both agree on." As they both reach Pier 10, Mayor Alvarez is already waiting. They exchange greetings. A slow-moving boat is headed in their direction; as it approaches them, it docks in front, and a large man, about six feet tall, bald, and about 45 years old, calls out, "Good morning, Juan, how are you?" "Great, Daren. I was under the impression this was a private meeting." Daren explains, "Let's get on board and get into the bay, and I will explain it to you, ok?" As they all climb on board the 30-footer, Dean remarks, "I am not much of a fisherman, your honor, but this is a beautiful boat." The Mayor answers, "You know, Detective, some guys love cars. Daren is crazy about boats. This is his baby." "Your honor, what is the name of the boat?" "Little Brooklyn, which is where he grew up, Brooklyn, NY." Daren hears the conversation and simply turns around and smiles at them. As he tries to enjoy the scenery, twenty minutes quickly go by, and the humming of the engine stops. You can hear the noise of the anchor dropping.

They slowly walk up to me, and as the Mayor approaches, he turns to the Captain, "Let me introduce Captain Flynn and Detective Dean." He reminds the gentleman, "First, let's get the ground rules in place. Juan, how do you know the Mayor?" "Juan and I have known each other for over thirty years. We were friends in college and law school. Our basic rule that we always adhere to throughout our friendship has been that under no circumstances have we ever lied to each other. It is our golden rule."

"All I want is an upfront evaluation of what you have, and I am sure it must be important to both of us, or else Juan would not have scheduled this meeting in the middle of Miami Bay, so let's get to it." Captain Flynn gives Daren a general overview picture because our meeting was important. The Mayor then explains to him why detective Dean was involved, and the Mayor also explains to him why he had to get involved. "By the way, gents, Daren is the Bureau Head of the Miami area DEA office." "Thank you for the intro, but how does this involve my office?" The Mayor asks Dean to explain to Daren what he has uncovered during his investigation. Dean explains to Daren how during the investigation and through a lengthy interview with Grace Pastore, he discovered the involvement of one of his undercover agents, Paige Green. As he gets to Paige's name, Daren gets out of his chair and starts to curse, "That son of a bitch!" Dean is startled by his outburst and momentarily stunned by his reaction. Daren catches his breath, apologizes for interrupting him, and asks Dean to continue. Dean further explains what they feel they have to do in order to bring this case to a final conviction of all the parties involved and, most importantly, to keep this case with as few people involved to make sure there are no leaks anywhere down the line. Dean completes his presentation, and Daren turns to Juan and remarks, "As usual Juan, you are always keeping me in the loop." The Mayor asks Daren, "Give us the lowdown on how the DEA first got involved." Daren starts to explain that

Paige was always a favorite of his because she graduated from our university. Juan and I had a common interest in her as she was smart, beautiful, and fearless in her approach to her job, and for the record, which was not her real name, but let's speak of her as Paige Green. The important thing is that, for the last two years or so, she was extracting great information, but for the last six months, we noticed that her personality was drastically changing. She was becoming more erratic and moodier, so when she got sick with a bad case of bronchitis, she had to be hospitalized. After a few tests were taken, we realized that we had a problem, and after her discharge, we had to keep a very close watch on her. During her stay, her boyfriend usually visited her, and not until later did we find out that the boyfriend was the same person she was investigating. At that point, we found out that she was using cocaine. We confronted her, and it became an extremely big problem. Here, we have an undercover agent working on a case for the last two years who is using the goods and was getting out of control. We had less than a week before she was to be discharged from the hospital, and we became unsure if her cover was blown." He takes a deep breath, "A very hairy situation; what to do?" He continues, "After confronting her about her problem, we both agreed we needed a change, and I blame myself for not taking action immediately when she told me that she was in love with the man." "God damn it," he shouted, "I should have insisted on taking her off the case. I blame myself for her death. You could see he was extremely upset." The Mayor tries to calm Daren down, "Come on, Daren, you can't blame yourself for her death. It is one of the tragedies that happen with our screwed-up job." "I know, Juan, but it still hurts, and as you know, a few weeks later she was found dead in a local fire. I am grateful that this opportunity came up, so maybe I could put this case to rest. Now Juan, what can my office do to help you?" "Well, Daren, we need any and all the information that agent Green was able to gather during her two-year investigation." "I will turn that over to you Juan as soon as I get to my office. It is going to take a few days, no problem." "The other point is, Daren, we need you to get involved off the record with the DA about our contact Grace Pastore, who is coming up for bail hearing." "That should not be a problem because he needs my help in a case he is involved with, and we can help each other." "Well, guys, this is a great fishing day, and now I think we should cast our lines and try to catch a few fish." "Alright, let's try it. I know Juan loves to fish, but if you two are not interested, there is a cooler full of beer and soda, so help yourselves. And by the way, bring us up two cold ones." "No problem, sir." "While we are on the boat, call me Daren."

The day is turning out to be a very pleasant and relaxing experience. The Mayor and his friend are fishing and just hanging out like old friends having a few cold ones, laughing, and just enjoying each other's company. Daren remarks to the Captain, "There are sandwiches down here. Do you want one?" "No, thank you. I don't want to embarrass myself by vomiting." Daren and the Captain just try to relax, and the only thing to do is try to get a suntan. The trip turns into a very relaxing afternoon of sunshine and an occasional brief nap. Hour's pass, and the Mayor and Daren are laughing at us sleeping, "Ok boys, it's time to head back." "How was the fishing?" "Not very good." "Lots of bites but no results?"

As they head home, Dean is just enjoying his surroundings. Finally, they head into the dark side areas and slowly approach their destination. Daren yells to Dean, "When we get close enough, jump off and tie the boat up, ok?" Dean watches intensely to make sure he does not fall in, and finally, the boat is close enough. He jumps on the dock and starts to tie it down. Daren yells, "Good job!" In the meantime, Captain Flynn seems very anxious to get back on solid ground, so he is the first one out. One by one, everyone is off, and as they gather, Daren thanks them for the informative meeting. He extends his hand to the Captain and Dean, shakes them, and then hugs his good friend, the Mayor, "Juan, I will be in touch." They all walk their separate ways, and the Mayor stops and calls Captain Flynn, "Captain, I will call you Monday. Have a good weekend." "Thank you, sir."

CHAPTER 6

Dean is tired after a long day on the water. He cannot wait to get home and go to bed. The next day cannot come soon enough. He must get everything ready for his dinner with Mary. First thing after breakfast, he starts to make sure the house is clean and sets the table for two. Looking in every drawer for candle holders and candles, he is running around the house, making sure everything is just perfect. Dean wants to impress Mary; he decides on the menu, and he is ready. The day passes swiftly, and before you know it, he runs upstairs to shower, shave, and get dressed. He walks into the living room, finds some smooth, romantic music, and loads it in his CD player. Everything is perfect, and the food is almost ready. Mary will arrive within the hour. He gives the house a final once-over, and it is all looking great. The doorbell rings, and he walks quickly to answer. He opens the door, and he just can't believe how beautiful Mary looks, "Come on in, and welcome to my house." He reaches over and kisses her. Mary hands Dean a bottle of red wine. "What is this?" "A little vino to go with our meal." "Thank you!" He escorts her into the living room, and Mary remarks, "Boy, Dean, you really did a nice job with this house." "Thank you. It took me long enough, but it is worth it now." "I can really consider it my house." "Mary, sit down, and I will open the wine." He goes into the kitchen, opens the bottle, and walks into the living room with wine glasses. "Hold on a minute," he runs back into the kitchen and grabs a bouquet of daisies. As he walks back, he makes sure they are hiding behind his back. He reaches near her and gives them to her. "Oh Dean, my favorite flowers! How did you know?"

"Come on Mary, it was easy. All over your desk, you have pencil holders, picture frames, all daisies. It was easy." "Come over here. It is really sweet of you." She gives him another kiss. He pours the wine and remarks that he would like to make a toast, "Salute amor y dinero." "What does that mean?" "It is an old Spanish toast – Love, Health and Wealth." "Very nice, but I would be satisfied with love and health Dean." They toast their glasses and take a sip. They continue the small talk; you could tell by the whole atmosphere that sparks are flying between them. Dean gets up, "Let me check on dinner before I burn it." He quickly looks and comes over; dinner is served. She gets up, and he helps her with her chair and starts to serve. "Mary, our favorite Caesar salad." "Beautiful table, Dean, let me light the candles." Dinner goes on with the same tempo as in a good restaurant. Each course is served, and there is good conversation, smiles, and laughter between them; every so often they exchange food from each other's plate, only stopped by the occasional kiss. "Dean, this is a great dinner you cooked." "Mary, when you are a bachelor, you better learn to cook, or you will starve." "Any more surprises, Dean?" "Well, it's dessert time!" He goes into the kitchen and brings out flan. Mary is taken aback, "Oh my god! Don't tell me you made this dessert." "Sure did. It was my mother's favorite, and she taught me how to make it." "Dean, this is awesome!" "Mary, don't tell me your mom is not a good cook." "She is, but it's the atmosphere we are in." "I guess you are right Mary. Either way, I am glad you really enjoyed it." Dinner is over, and he goes over and helps her with her chair. They both walk into the living room. Soft romantic music is playing, and Mary holds Dean's hand and says, "Let's dance." As they embrace tightly and begin to dance, it is not long before they are both kissing each other passionately. A few more moves, and they continue to kiss. The atmosphere is surrounded by love and passion. Dean finally picks up Mary in his arms and carries her up the stairs; they're still kissing each other. As the morning sun starts to shine through the window, they wake up, look at each other, and Mary tells Dean what a wonderful evening she had. Dean reaches over, gives Mary another long kiss, and asks her what she wants for breakfast. She simply tells him, "It's your choice." He quickly runs in the bathroom, washes up, and runs downstairs to the kitchen feeling very happy, with a new bounce in his step. He makes her eggs, bacon, toast, orange juice, and coffee and brings it upstairs. "Now it is my turn, and we can enjoy it together." Dean tells Mary in the bathroom that he has a new toothbrush she can use. They have their breakfast and continue to talk, and Mary tells Dean that last week, Lieutenant Max called Captain Flynn, and she overheard the Captain telling him not to interfere with their investigation, and if it continues, he would be hearing from the Mayor's office. The Captain told Lieutenant Max that he would be advised at the proper time; he was not very happy, but he realized he better play the game. Also, the Captain told him that he has a meeting with Police Commissioner Alicia on Tuesday afternoon. She has no idea what that was all about, and Dean, too, did not have a clue.

"Dean, what are you going to do the rest of the weekend?" "Just finish up some of the unfinished little projects left with this house. How about you Mary?" I have a family party tonight, and on Sunday, I am just going to relax. Dean, thank you for a great evening." They kiss, and he starts to take the dishes downstairs. "Dean, I am going to take a quick shower, get dressed, and head home, ok?" "I will be downstairs waiting for you." Twenty minutes go by, Mary comes in the kitchen, and Dean is having his second cup of coffee. "Dean, I am leaving." "Let me walk you to the front door." "I will call you." He watches her get into her car and pull away. He just can't stop thinking about what just happened between them, and he really feels good about his relationship with her.

Bright and early, on Monday morning, Dean gets up and gets ready for his morning run. He can tell he is getting in better shape because he is enjoying the morning run with little or no aches and pains. He completes his workout, showers, gets dressed, and out the door he goes. No sooner he starts his car, his cell phone rings and it's the Captain, "How was your weekend?" "Good, thank you." "Look, Dean, meet me at Gavin's corner deli. Do you know where it is?" "Sure, Captain." "Go straight in the back, and I will be waiting for you, ok?" Dean thinks, "Something must be up if the Captain called me at home and asked me to meet him outside the office." He starts his trip wondering all along about this meeting. He finally arrives, parks, and walks toward the back, where Captain Flynn sees him and waves him to come sit down. The server comes over, "What can I bring you?" Dean orders coffee, and Captain Flynn tells her, "Make that two, thank you." He tells Dean about the phone conversation with Lt. Max and the tone of voice he had to use to make his point. Dean asks, "Do you think he was satisfied with your answer?" "I really don't give a shit what he thinks. I told him in no uncertain words either to get out of the way, or he is going to answer to the Mayor. He quickly changed his tone and told me he was at our disposal. I thanked him and told him that I would fill him in at the right time." Captain Flynn hands Dean a yellow manilla envelope and tells him all the information that the DEA has on the pending case that Agent Paige accumulated. He then tells Dean that he has already read all the info and advised him to go home and study the contents. By the time coffee arrives, Captain Flynn says to Dean, "When you finish the case file, call me and we will discuss the additional help we need, possibly Sergeant Scott. I have a meeting with the police commissioner on Wednesday morning, and I will further touch base with him. The Mayor already covered the move with him, so I don't see any trouble at all. Listen, enjoy your coffee, and call me later." "Thank you, Captain."

Dean can't swallow his coffee fast enough, calls the waitress over, pays the bill, and out he goes. As he starts driving home, he decides to call Sergeant Scott. Within a few rings, the phone is answered, "Scotty, how in the hell are you?" "Just fine, Dean." "Just listen Scotty, do you remember I told you I was going to use you for a case?" "Yes, I recall our conversation." "By the end of the week, I feel you and I will be back as partners. I will explain at the proper time." "Listen Dean, don't pull my chain." "No shit, I would not be telling you if I didn't mean it, so hang in and I will be in touch. Keep your mouth shut." "No problem, Dean." "And thanks again, see you soon Scotty."

Home, at last. He sits down on a chair and opens the Manila envelope. It contains pictures of different locations, and one of them looks very familiar. There are pictures of Cooper, the suspect, and a complete police breakdown on him. The more he reads, the more he realizes that Cooper has no scruples. He will do anything for money. This guy has been in trouble since the age of fourteen, deeper in crimes as he gets older—prostitution, drugs, stolen goods, illegal transportation of people. One very important point is that he has always been able to make bail, and the same company might be his source of unlimited money. He has quite a few associates with local drug families. One can see that he is not a choir member. Hours of reading go by, and his rap sheet is very interesting. Great reading, but it makes Dean realize that he stops at nothing to achieve his goal, and nothing stops him—a very calm and collective psychopath, dangerous. Dean thinks to himself, "I better call Captain Flynn." "Hello, Dean. What's your opinion of our boy Cooper?" "Dangerous and stops at nothing." "Listen, after my meeting with the Chief of Police, I want you to meet me at my office to talk about the plan of attack with this case, and also bring Sergeant Scott." "Great, Captain! I will wait for your call."

CHAPTER 7

Dean thinks to himself, "Life is looking up for me, and I have to take advantage of my opportunity". As the day quickly passes, I am more involved in this information in front of me and still trying to find a weak point in his character that we can use to our advantage. Let me get to bed. It's two o'clock in the morning; off to bed and tomorrow is another day. Up early and out jogging all along the two-mile run, all he can think about is the right approach to the upcoming situation. Every episode in his life is about money and power, so he will have to appeal to his ambition, greed, and power hunger. He runs upstairs to shower and gets ready for the meeting with the Captain. No sooner, the phone in the kitchen rings. He looks at his cell phone, and it is Mary. He quickly answers, "Good morning, beautiful." "Hi Dean, the latest news from the rumor mill is that Captain Flynn is going to be promoted to Mayor." "Which is great news, Mary, he really deserves it." "He is on his way back, so keep it under your hat. It's really great news. Let me get off the phone. I hear someone opening the door." "Good morning, Captain, are you ok? You look kind of pale." He looks up and tells Mary, "You are not going to believe this. I am being promoted to Mayor. I still can't believe it." "Sit down and let me get you a cup of coffee." "Thank you, I can really use it." "Captain, can you tell me about it?" "Sure, Mayor Tolley is retiring at the end of the month because of health reasons, and to my surprise, I was one of four candidates for the job. The Police Commissioner, along with the Mayor, felt that I was the best candidate for the vacancy. I still can't believe it. I am going in my office to try and relax for a few minutes, and please call detective Dean and tell him to come in." "Ok Captain, or should I say Mayor?" A very big smile appears on his face. Mary calls Dean to inform him that the rumor was correct and that he wants him in ASAP. Dean arrives, parks, and quickly walks to the front door. As usual, a smiling Sergeant Garcia greets him, "Detective, come over here." "Listen, Dean, it seems everyone you come in contact with sooner or later gets promoted. How about a good word for Garcia?" Dean smiles, "Listen, Sergeant, you're the best front desk Sergeant in the department. Why would I want to get rid of your smiling face?" "Come on Dean, give me a break," he smiles, and Dean quickly walks down the hall to the Captain's office. "Hello, Mary. Where is our new Mayor?" "In his office. Let me tell him you are here." "Not before I give you a kiss." "Sir, Dean is here." "Send him in." "I just heard the good news, Sir." "I still can't believe it Dean." "I don't want to get mushy with you, sir, but because of your help, guidance, and understanding, I have been able to get my life back in order and feel that I have a future. As far as I am concerned, you deserve a promotion. Let's look at it as a reward for 25 years of honest police work. You are admired by your peers. So let me be the first to congratulate you, and my father is sure to be looking down with a smile on his face for you. I would like to give you my father's gold leaves, and I hope you wear them when you are promoted. It would be my honor."

To Dean's surprise, or maybe it was his imagination, the old man had a tear in his eye. He extended his hand to Dean and grabbed it so hard that for a moment Dean felt it was going to be fractured. "Congrats, Mayor." "Not yet, Dean." "How did all of this come about?" "Mayor Tolley, who heads the special investigation unit, is retiring for health reasons, so the vacancy opened up, and I was one of four candidates. To my surprise, they picked me." "Again, you deserve it." "So, that means Lieutenant Max is working for you now." "Holy shit, he is in for a surprise."

Dean can't stop laughing. "What is so funny, Dean?" "I just can't wait to see the look on his face when he hears the news." Flynn smiles.

"Well, Dean, let's get down to business. Let's talk about our approach to solving the problem that we face. Have you read his complete file?" "Yes Captain, and I feel we have to find out his sources because he covers his bases very thoroughly and really doesn't trust anyone. I feel our best approach is Grace Pastore. One glaring fact is that every time he needed help posting the bond, the same company showed up." "What is so strange about that Dean? This is how they make their money." "It is a company from Jacksonville area. Why would they travel all that distance?" "You may have a point. Let's research them and see what we come up with to start." "Captain, have you heard from the DA's office?" "Yes, special agent Daren called and told me that he spoke to the DA, and it's a go. The next thing is to give Grace Pastore the news and set up the sting. "How do you know she is going to go along?" "She really has no choice. Either she cooperates or faces jail time. I will make all of the arrangements to have Sergeant Scott transferred to our unit as of Monday, and I want you to fill him in and start using him. From now on, I need weekly contact on progress without fail. I will give you my private cell number for an additional contact point. I am going to meet my department heads next week, and I will cover our operation with Lieutenant Max. This time he will not hesitate to just listen and cooperate, or I will have his ass."

"Grace Pastore's bail hearing is set for next week, so you better get to her quickly." "No problem, Captain." He walks out of the office and over to Mary. "I will call you later." He kisses her and walks out. As he starts walking down the hall, Lieutenant Max walks out of his office and is surprised to see him. "Dean, I just heard the rumor." "It's no rumor, Lieutenant. Our new boss is Captain Flynn. I mean Mayor Flynn." He takes a deep breath, "I really have to talk to him." "Lieutenant, let me give you a heads up. Hold on; he is going to see you next week." He looks up with a surprised look on his face, "Are you sure?" "Believe me, hold on." "Thank you, Dean, have a good day." He walks past Sergeant Garcia, who gives him a wave. He walks down to his car, gets in, and calls Scotty. "Hi Dean." "What's up, Scotty? After your shift, come to my house, and I will explain everything to you." "Great, Dean. I should be there around five o'clock. I will bring us a couple of Cuban sandwiches, my treat." "Great! I have plenty of beer, so we are all set."

Dean gets home, changes his clothes, and tries to calm down and relax until his meeting with Scott. What a better way to relax than to call Mary. Their conversation lasted over 20 minutes. She finally tells Dean it's a good thing the Captain is out of the office or else he would have started screaming. "Look, Dean, I will come over tomorrow night, and this time I will bring dinner." "Ok, see you tomorrow."

Dean is mentally drained. He sits on the living room couch, and before you know it, he is out like a light. He feels like he is in a dream, and the doorbell wakes him up. Scott is at the door. "Dean, in here! Where have you been? I have been ringing the bell for ten minutes." "I fell asleep on the couch." "You better splash some water on your face, and let's sit down to eat. I am starving." "Scott, you are always starving. Come in the kitchen, and we can eat and talk." Scott starts to empty the paper bags. Dean remarks, "You have enough food to feed an army." "Just shut up and get the beer." "Scotty, first things first, as of Monday the Captain, or should I say Mayor Flynn, will officially call you in his office and put you in plain clothes for working with me on a case that I have been on for the past six months. Let me just make sure you understand the situation. I am basically working for the Mayor and Captain Flynn." "What do you mean Mayor Flynn?" "Captain Flynn at the of the month will be the new boss of the special investigation unit. Lieutenant Max's department is one of his responsibilities. Getting back to the Mayor, as you remember, there have been six mysterious fires in the Miami area, and the Mayor has been under quite a bit of pressure to solve the problem, so Captain Flynn suggested forming an investigation team to try to solve the problem. The reason I was able to get you transferred is that I made it a point to tell them about your cooperation with Grace Pastore." Scott looks puzzled. "Whether you realize it or not, you are getting together with her was the turning point." "How does she fit in with all of this?" "I will explain it to you. When I interviewed her at the detention center, she gave up one of the players involved. You know this piece of shit, Cooper? That creep has been involved in drugs, prostitution, you name it. That is our connection to the case, and the studio is owned by our very own Mr. Cooper." "Dean, I could never figure out how a street punk like him became so rich and powerful." "That is where you come in. Your job is going to keep track of our girl, Grace. Grow a beard and do what you have to, but make sure she doesn't recognize you." "Dean, we already have a problem. I have a yellow jeep, and it sticks out like a sore thumb." "We can take care of that. I am sure Captain Flynn can find you a car from a previous drug bust." "But Dean, she is in the lock up." "Her hearing is next week, and she will make bail. First, I want you to ask around about the bail company that Cooper used every time he was busted. They are from the Jacksonville area. I think the coincidence with them, and our boy is just too cozy."

"I am going to see her this week and give her a choice to either cooperate or go to jail." "Dean, I can't believe you would trust that bitch." "Scotty, we have to play the cards that are handed to us, and by the way, you remember my old girlfriend, Paige?" "I remember. Wasn't she found in one of the fires?"" Yes, she was. She was an undercover agent for the DEA." "Are you kidding me? This sounds like a Hollywood movie." "It's the real thing Scotty. We have our hands full, so you really have to keep your mouth shut, watch your ass, and keep your ears open. Finish up your dinner, and I will show you all the info we have on our boy, Cooper." "Dean, before we go any further, thank you for bringing me in on this." "Listen, Scotty, we have had our differences since the police academy, but you have always been there for me, in good or bad times, and I can always count on you." "Thanks, Dean. Believe me, I won't let you down. Getting off the subject lover boy, rumor has it that you and Mary are pretty close." "Yes, we are. She is really good for me, and we have a lot in common, and like you she really looks out for me." "Great, Dean! As long as you are happy, that is all that matters."

"Look over all of the information on the dining room table and see what can be helpful to us. I will tell you one thing, Scotty, I did not realize how connected all of the people are with the Mayor. You're on his team, and boy he can really help you. He just got re-elected, so for at least the next four years, we are on the right team. Let me make sure you understand the chain of command. All info is funneled through me, and I will make the Captain aware of all situations. Under no circumstance, and I mean not once, if confronted by Lieutenant Max or anyone else, you are to say anything to anyone. If confronted, you just say 'Sorry, no comment, talk to detective Dean.' Be polite, but don't take any shit. Do you understand me loud and clear? Play dumb when the Captain calls you in on Monday and then get back to me. Make all of your calls to my cell phone, and I will do the same. If I don't answer, don't leave any messages; just say, 'Dean call me,' understand? I will keep you well informed of my progress to make sure that we are both travelling the same road. The first move I have to do is go visit Grace at the detention center tomorrow, and we will talk as soon as I finish with her. In the meantime, act surprised when you interview with the Captain, but don't act stupid. Ok, Scotty, let's call it a night. I am tired and want to hit the sack early tonight." "Thanks again, Dean, and thanks again for the opportunity." "Don't mention it. Take care."

Up early and out the door early for my morning jog. These days, my two-mile run seems to be easier as each day goes on. A good sign for a guy who would be out of breath just walking around the block eight months ago.

CHAPTER 8

HOME SWEET HOME. MORNING TRAFFIC SEEMS REALLY HEAVY. THE half-hour drive to the detention center looks like it's going to take me at least an hour. Finally, arriving check-in is becoming second nature: walk through the gated area into the main office, show my ID, check my firearm, and sign the book. As usual, Sergeant Lisa greets me, "Morning, Detective. Would you like a cup of coffee?" "That would be great, Sergeant." "Detective, use your room 10 and I will call for Grace Pastore." "I always figured you for a mind reader, Sergeant," he laughs. "It is part of the job," she replies. She hands me my coffee, and I walk down the hall to the interrogation room. As I sit down and take a sip of coffee, Grace comes with an officer. The officer asks me, "Would you like me to stay?" "No, that's ok. Just wait outside." Grace waits for the officer to leave the room and gives me a big smile. "Hi Dean, how are you?" "Just fine, Grace. I checked out the info you gave me, and you were on the money." "I told you Dean, no bullshit. I know what I am talking about. Can you help me Dean?" "I think we can do some business, Grace." She seems very relieved and excited with the news. "Grace, you have to realize I am really gambling with my career trusting you, so you better not disappoint me." "No Dean, I will do whatever you want." "Grace, just listen to me. Your bail hearing is scheduled for next Tuesday at 10 in the morning. A police defender has been assigned to you by the name of Ty Elgin. He will represent you and tell you that he is going to ask the judge for a bail setting of $100,000." "Wow Dean, that's great!" "Just act grateful and surprised. What I want you to do is, after you meet with him, call Cooper and tell him you need his help to make the bail. He has a connection with a bail bondsman from Jacksonville." "You mean Jake's Bond Supreme?" "How do you know them, Grace?" "He is involved with Cooper one way or another. I had to call him for Cooper a couple of times." "Cooper will be curious as to how your bail is so low, since all of those charges were filed against you. Ask your attorney Ty why he is asking for such a low bail amount, and he will explain to you. It is because, with eight other persons involved, the police have not been able to pinpoint all the drugs on one person, so they are just trying to look good and hoping someone screws up and rats on the rest. Grace, it is extremely important that you communicate with me after you speak to your attorney, and especially after you talk to Cooper." "Believe me Dean, I will call after I speak to both of them." "If everything goes well, you will be a free woman by next Tuesday afternoon." "Dean, believe me, you won't be sorry." "Talk is cheap, Grace. I am counting on you." He gets up and knocks on the door. The officer tells Grace to get up, and both of them walk out. The first part of the plan was implemented. Now starts the most delicate part to make sure she continues to cooperate and starts to become more crucial to Cooper's organization. He checks out of the center, and as soon as he gets into his car, he contacts Captain Flynn and informs him of the conversation with Grace. He also tells him about the bail bonds company involved, so that when he meets with Lieutenant Max, he may be able to shed some light on their operations.

"You know, Dean, I think it is about time I get Lieutenant Max involved." "I think you are right, Captain, but just a suggestion that he should understand how delicate this matter is and that the info you give him stays with him only. This way, he will feel you have confidence in his ability, since you are or will be his new boss." "Good point, Dean. And by the way, Sergeant Scott is coming in to see me." "Thank you, Captain." "Mary, at what time is Sergeant Scott scheduled to meet me today?" "4:00, Captain." "Good, Mary. I have a few stops to make today, so I will be out of the office, but will be back in time for my meeting. If I receive any important phone calls, you know how to reach me."

Dean is consumed with the information given to him about Cooper. It's like reading a book he can't seem to put down; it's becoming an obsession with him. The only thing that breaks his concentration is his phone ringing. He answers, "Hello Scott, what is going on?" "I just had my interview with the Captain, and he explained to me about the special investigation unit. He told me that, based on your recommendation, he assigned me to the unit, and I was told to report to you for instructions. I thanked him and his last words to me were, 'Don't fuck it up, or I will be back on the street in uniform again.' Thanks, Dean." No problem, Scotty. Meet me at my house later on today, and I will fill you in on the operation." No sooner he gets off the phone with Scott, he receives another call. This time, it's Grace. She sounds very excited. She goes on to explain that what they spoke about is exactly what is going to be presented to the judge, and that he sees no reason why she would not be able to get out if the bail is posted. Dean tries to calm her down and again makes her realize the importance of her calling Cooper for help. "Grace, you better put forward your best acting performance if you want to get out." "Don't worry Dean, I will make it good, and I will be in touch. Thanks again." Things seem to be falling in place. Dean just didn't want to get too full of himself because he knows that when you are dealing with such a case, its survival first and commitment last. The only thing in his favor if Grace does not cooperate, her ass will be back in jail quickly, and they spread the rumor that she is an informant. The doorbell rings, and it is Scott." Come on in, Scotty." "Dean, I have to compliment you." "What happened man? What in hell do you mean?" "Don't play innocent with me, Dean. Not too long ago, you would have been happy to have the brass speak to you; now, they ask for your opinion and suggestions." "I can't explain it, Scotty. It's just luck and just a little bit of connections." "Well, brother, I am just glad I know you." "Ok, enough of the bullshit. Let's get us a beer and sit down. Let me explain the situation. I will bring you up to date on all the meetings and people involved." Scott seems amazed at the involvement of the operation. He remarks, "You mean to tell me that Lt. Max is completely in the dark about this?" "Yes, that should make you realize the importance of our operation. Captain Flynn will be informing him sometime this week when he has his department meeting about it, but like I told you before, it's to be discussed only with each other, and if any information is obtained, I will give it to Captain Flynn. Do I make myself clear?" "No problem, Dean." "The first thing on the agenda is that you are to work as a freelancer, pull all your favors, check with your connections, and start to try and find out as much as possible about our friend Cooper and as discretely as possible. No one in the department knows your new position. The word is that your butt is on paid department leave pending a board review. That is your cover. When you leave home, go to the impound yard and pick out any car you need. They will not ask any questions, and when you need to communicate with me, you know what to do. You have a few days until you start, so try to relax." "Why a few days?" "Our girl Grace will come up for her bail hearing on Tuesday, and when she is released, stay on her like a rash, she is going to be our key lead." "Ok Dean, things are happening so fast my head is spinning." "Just take a few days off to focus on your job." "By the way, Dean, Captain Flynn told me that my future depends on my performance." "Scotty, one thing I found out about Captain Flynn is that he takes care of people. Hold on Scotty. Let me get this phone call. It's Grace." "Everything is a go, Dean. We had a long conversation, Cooper and I, and he seemed pleased about the potential bail release and told me he would make sure the bail was no problem. But he also told me he felt that I seemed to be a person who could be trusted and that he was going to give me further responsibilities when I got out. I told him he could count on me. I must get off the phone, talk to you as soon as I get out." "Good luck, Grace." The excitement of staging, planning, and putting the complete project to work consumed Dean, and the days passed like preparing for finals; you can't wait to take the test and check out all your hard work. That's the way Dean was trying to approach this assignment. It was different, but, in many ways, rewarding. Dean picks up his cell phone and calls Mary. After a few rings, she answers, "Hello stranger," "It is not by choice Mary. I have been so busy getting everything ready that I did not have the time, but believe me, you are always with me." She clears her throat, "Well, good looking, if you have the time, why don't we go out for a drink tonight?" "That's great." "Dean, pick me up around seven o'clock." "Ok, see you then."

Dean realizes what an important part of his life Mary has become. After this situation is taken care of, I have to make it a priority to include Mary in my life, something I never thought was possible. I answer my cell phone, and Grace's voice is filled with excitement. She can't stop thanking me for helping her, and I had to calm her down and explain to her again that her job is only just starting and that it's important for her to keep her guard up at all times. I also strongly reminded her that when you deal with a person like Cooper, you better be on top of your game; it's a matter of survival. She took a deep breath and agreed with me. "Grace, enjoy the rest of your day, and I will be in touch with you soon." "Thank you, Dean!" He dials Captain Flynn, "Good afternoon, Captain. Grace's release went smoothly, and everything is in place. Sergeant Scott has been given his assignment, and he understands it completely. I will call Grace tomorrow and contact her only via cell phone, just for the time being." "I think that is a good approach, Dean." "I will keep you well aware of the situation, Captain." "Ok Dean, and by the way, I had my meeting with Lieutenant Max. He was impressed with the way this sting was planned and implemented. He will start on his end to try to help as much as he can. I also made it a point to again point out the importance of complete silence at this time, and he understood. He thanked me for having confidence in him to include his services in the operation. I further explained why it was being done in this manner, and he completely agreed. What else was he going to say? If you want to survive, you do not argue with the boss."

I called Scotty, explained to him about Grace getting out of jail, and asked him to start with Grace on Monday. He told me that he is starting as of today; he can't wait and just hang around. Grace clears all her judicial hurdles, and within a few hours of her court hearing, she is back in Miami. First things first, I need a drink, and what better place than her old hangout, the Bolero Bar. As she is greeted, she feels at home. She sits at the bar, just enjoying her new freedom, and to her surprise, she is surprised by her boss. "Oh my god, Cooper! It didn't take you long to catch up with me," Grace remarks. "We try to take care of our own, Grace." She was surprised to hear that and experienced a feeling she had never felt before. "Thank you, Cooper." "Just enjoy yourself, and I will drop by to see you on Monday." "Thanks, Cooper." "Just behave." "She laughs out loud, "Sure, after what I have been through, I am going to have a good steak, buy myself a bottle of rum, catch up with my old friend and just enjoy." Cooper laughs and waves goodbye. Grace just continues to enjoy herself and her drinks. The night flies by, and the only change that happened to Grace was that she was getting more drunk. Finally, she has had enough. She tips the bartender and slowly walks out the door. Thank goodness, her old apartment is only a few blocks away. Slowly and wobbly, she finally arrives at her door and fumbles for her key. Slowly, she gets the door open and walks inside the place. As always, it has this old musty smell, but it is home. She stumbles into her room and falls into bed. It feels simply great to finally fall asleep in a normal surrounding, no noise or screams, just peace and quiet. The morning comes so fast. As she opens her eyes momentarily, she has not yet realized that she is free. Her eyes wander all over the room, and finally, it sinks in that she is out of jail. She takes a deep breath, and for the first time, it's great to be free. She slowly gets up, still a little apprehensive, and changes her clothing and walks into the kitchen. To her surprise, the refrigerator is full, and coffee is in the cabinet. A nice feeling comes over her, "Wow, I better not get too full of myself, or the next move could be looking down." It's been a long time since she was able to make herself a breakfast of her choice, and she slowly enjoys such small pleasures. As she starts to clean up, Cooper's voice startles her. "Man, Cooper. You scared the hell out of me."

Officer Scott has been keeping an eye on Grace since her release and decides to check in with Dean. He calls, and his call is quickly answered, "Morning Scotty, what is up?" "Everything so far is going nice and normal Dean, but we both know this chick is as slippery as an eel." "Scotty, I have been thinking along those lines. I am going to call the Captain, and maybe we both can come up with a safe way to really keep up with her so that you can keep your distance and don't spook her." "Great Dean, I will keep in touch." After he hangs up the phone, Dean starts to think seriously about what he and Scotty talked about. He calls Captain Flynn's office to try and set up an appointment. "Captain Flynn's office," the familiar voice of Mary is at the other end. "Hello, good looking." "Hello yourself." "Dean, how are you?" "Just fine, thank you for a great dinner Thursday night." "I am so glad you enjoyed it." "And dessert was spectacular." "Stop, you are making me blush." "Mary, can you set you an appointment with the boss?" "Hold on Dean, the Captain is calling me." A few minutes go by and Mary returns, "You do not have to wait. The Captain wants to see you on Friday morning at 8:00 sharp." "Thanks, Mary, and by the way, would you like to go to brunch on Sunday morning?" "That would be great! Saturday night, I have a birthday party at my cousin's house. He is only eight years old." "Enjoy it! See you Sunday morning." Grace gave him a lead on a company, an import and export company. But no one seemed to know much about them. As he looks through his notes, he comes across Panama Imports, Panama City, Panama. He could surely check all ship arrivals at the port. It would just take a little work, and then he could find out which ships come directly into Miami. Thank God for today's laptops, only a few hours of work, and he lists all commercial ships that have docked in Miami straight from Panama. The next thing is to find the cargo manifest. Slowly, he begins to see a pattern. Every month, GI Importing Company delivers crates of canvas to the same corporation, and to his amazement, it is to a Jake's Supreme Warehousing services out of Jacksonville. Why Miami and not Jacksonville? His mind is starting to run wild with excitement. He thinks to himself, "Computer, do not fail me now!" Jake's Supreme Warehouse Services has a cheese import company and ten pizza shops spread all over the Miami metropolitan area. He starts to think back about the information that Grace gave him about the GI crates at the studio: one day in the storage area, then gone. But he remembers her curiosity about the white sugary powder on the floor. He gets on the phone and calls Scotty; in a few minutes, he answers. "Scotty in your time on the street, have you ever heard any rumors about GI Importing Company?" "No, but I will call a few of my contacts and get back to you." "Call as soon as you hear anything." "What's up, Dean?" "Just a hunch, just a hunch." It's really making Dean think, and he's back on the internet. More digging, and the longer he looks, the more the whole picture starts to form. He starts connecting the dots together, "It's an amazing scheme, a genius approach. Just a hunch, a suspicion, but it really is a genius plan—kudos to the organization. We are dealing with a person or persons who took time to lay out this whole scheme and left nothing to chance. In my opinion, the only thing that can tear it down is greed. I am putting my money on Cooper; he is the one person who could lead me to payout." Dean's head has been spinning for the last few days, and so many scenarios are popping into his head that he can't wait to see Captain Flynn. The morning can't come soon enough.

He is so uptight with his theories that he does not even eat breakfast, gets dressed quickly, and off he goes to see Captain Flynn. He does not realize that his meeting with the boss is at 8:00. It finally hits him when he reaches the station parking lot. He looks at his watch, and it's only 7:00. He starts to laugh, parks his car, drops his parking plaque on his dash, and slowly walks to the station. He opens the door; not even the ever-smiling Sergeant Garcia is at his post. Dean just walks down the hall and knocks at the Captain's door, walks in, and calls out for Mary. As she peeks around the wall, she says, "Wow, Dean. You sure are early." "I just lost track of time." Mary walks over, and she gives him an embrace and a kiss. "What is that all about?" "Just a nice gesture for a beautiful woman." Mary blushes. "Go sit down, and I will bring you a cup of coffee." "Thank you, Mary." As they enjoy the morning coffee, Captain Flynn walks in and is surprised to see them both just enjoying each other's company; he just smiles. "Mary, could you please give me my usual?" "No problem, Captain." She quickly gets up and brings him his morning coffee. "Give me a few minutes and then send in Dean."

"Morning, Captain." "How are you Dean?" "Just fine." "Bring me up to date on our investigation." "Sergeant Scott has been on the street conducting surveillance of Grace, and to date, not too much activity. She has been in contact with me and informs me of monthly shipments from Panama containing display and art materials from the same company. I have tried to research them, and all I could find is an importing and exporting company based out of Jacksonville that has a few subsidiaries that deal in various things, from art supplies to cheese imports, and the latter does not fit because Panama is not known for cheese products. I have Scott checking his sources, but the strange thing is that Grace tells me she supervises monthly pickups from Panama and delivers them to a cheese processing plant in Miami to our friend Cooper." "Ok, Dean. We will figure that out. By the way, stick around. I have Lieutenant Max coming in to meet with us in a half hour." "Captain, have you filled him in on our operation?" "Last week, I met with him, and I explained to him the operation. He was happy to be part of it. He meets with me on a weekly basis, and we go over the ongoing street operations. He is very enthusiastic about his role; as a matter of fact, he should be arriving in ten minutes. Let's have a cup of coffee and wait for him." "Great, Captain." They get up and walk to the next room. Mary looks at Dean, and he just gives her a thumbs-up. "Mary, where is the coffee? We need to make another pot." "Don't bother Captain, just relax and I will take care of it." "Thanks! When it's ready please bring another cup. Lieutenant Max will be joining us." The door opens up, and Lieutenant Max walks in. "Good morning, all." "Well, let's go in my office. Take a seat, gents, and get comfortable." Captain Flynn fills in the Lieutenant on his previous conversations, and detective Dean gives a general presentation of what is going on and explains his research into GI deliveries at the port as well as his curiosity about GI importing cheese. The Lieutenant's face lights up, "Hold on a minute, Dean. That name rings a bell. Let me quickly go through my reports." As he nervously looks at his weekly booking reports, here it is a Mr. Nicholas Smith working for GI Imports who was stopped for running a traffic light. "No driver's license, and it turns out

that he is on a work release program from a local halfway house."
"How did he get involved with a traffic violation?" Lieutenant
Max continues, "It was just the luck of the officer who made the
stop. He noticed two containers of cheese on the front seat and
remarked, 'What's with the cheese?' 'I work for a cheese company
and was taking them home.' 'Is the cheese any good?' Nicholas
answered, 'We only make the best.' 'Well, let's have a taste.'
At this point, Mr. Smith became very nervous, and the officer
became uneasy with the situation. He asked Mr. Smith to get out
of the car, handcuffed him, and put him in the patrol car. His
curiosity got the best of him. He opened one of the containers
and began tasting the so-called cheese. The taste was nothing
like he had ever tasted. He rolled out his drug test kit, and to his
surprise, the cheese tested positive for cocaine. He took a deep
breath and called for backup. He explained the situation to the
Sergeant, and both of them realized this is more than meets the
eye. As they walked back to talk to Nicholas Smith, he was given
his Miranda rights, and all Mr. Smith kept on repeating was, 'I
am dead, I am dead. The officers asked, 'What the hell are you
talking about? This is how we got involved. He was still amazed at
the situation and was relieved when the watch supervisor arrived.
The officers searched him." "This is very helpful information,
Lieutenant. This may be our break into our whole operation."
Captain Flynn asks, "Where is he now?" "At the correctional
holding facility." As all parties were amazed at listening about the
bust, Mary walks in with coffee. "Great timing, Mary, we really
need a pause to think, and what better way than with a cup of
coffee." She puts the tray on the Captain's desk and walks away.
Captain Flynn realizes this opportunity, "Well boys, let's hear
some suggestions." Lieutenant Max is the first to speak. "Captain,
let's do a background on our perp and then question him for more
good info." "Good start. What about you Dean?" "I would like
to be present when Lieutenant Max does the questioning." Max

speaks up, "No problem, Dean. I just think after meeting with this person we should meet again and see what we come up with and then take action." "Ok, let's meet on Thursday at 8:00 am here and proceed from there." "Ok, see you guys. Dean, I will meet you tomorrow at the detention center at 9:00 a.m. I will start to dig up as much info on the suspect." "Ok Lieutenant, I will do the same." "Dean, here is his rap sheet." They all get up and walk out of the office. Dean gestures to Mary that he will call her later. As he walks out of the building, he picks up his cell and calls Scotty. "What's up, Dean?" "Scotty, meet me at my house tonight around 7:00." "Ok, is everything ok?" "I think we may finally have a lead that can help us." "Great, I will see you tonight. By the way, Dean, I will pick up a pizza, and this time you are paying." "No problem. See you later."

As Dean's mind thinks about the possible connections in the case, he starts to get ahead of himself. Thank God for the doorbell to break the tension. A smiling Scotty arrives with pizza. He can't wait to tell Scott the latest info. They both sit down, and Dean explains what happened at their meeting. Scott can't believe what he is hearing. "Scotty, this may be the opportunity we needed. Tomorrow, keep a closer eye on our girl, Grace. This may now start to open up now that we have one of the operators."

CHAPTER 9

LIEUTENANT MAX HAS BEEN NERVOUS AS HELL. IN HIS MIND, HE feels that this is the opportunity he has been waiting for throughout his law enforcement career. A contribution to the team, a potential step toward promotion. He finally realizes that first of all, he has to be a cop. He finally takes a deep breath and returns to reality. He calls his connection at the county lockup, Sergeant Lisa, and asks her to dig up all the information on Mr. Smith and to set up an interview room for tomorrow at 9:00 a.m.

Both Lieutenant Max and detective Dean wait anxiously for Mr. Smith to arrive in the interview room. As they have read his rap sheet, they know that he has had run-ins with the law, starting as young as fourteen years old, and the older he got, his crimes escalated in and out of jail. Finally, a knock on the door and a smiling Sergeant Lisa brings in Mr. Smith. Mr. Smith looks around the room and remarks, "The dynamic duo." Max and Dean are standing in the room as Sergeant Lisa delivers the prisoner, "I will be outside in the hallway?" Mr. Smith starts to panic. He realizes he is in deep shit and once again starts to recant, "I'm dead. I'm dead." To his surprise, both Lieutenant Max and Detective Dean burst out laughing. "What's so goddamn funny?" "At this point we have no idea what you are mumbling about." He takes a deep breath. "Ok, let me explain the situation I am in. As you may know by now, I live in a halfway house, and I was approached by another inmate prior to my release to ask if I was trustworthy and dependable. I was confused. What in the hell are they talking about? He told me not to ask any questions and to just listen. He explained that he could guarantee me a transfer to a halfway house if I agreed to certain conditions. His offer sounded too good. How could anyone with half a brain turn that offer down? My alternative was finishing up the rest of my sentence in jail. I didn't give it a second thought. I agreed, but somewhere felt I was handed a bullshit line by a jail con artist. Not until two weeks later, I realized it was all legit when I sat before the parole board, and after I played one of my best acting parts, I was informed that in two weeks, I was going to be transferred to a halfway house. My head was spinning, and I could not wait to see what in the hell was going on. Two weeks seemed an eternity, but finally, I was out of jail and in a halfway house—free but with a mindset of apprehension. After a few days, I was approached by one of the other inmates in residence, and they explained to me my work duties. I was told that I would be a pizza delivery man and would have to deliver pizzas and cheese at any time during the day and night to whatever address I was given." "So, how in hell did you get busted?" "Well, greed got the best of me. I made an unsanctioned delivery on my own." "Wait, explain what in the hell you are talking about." "G&I Imports has over 15 pizza shops in the Miami area. It's a perfect network for the distribution of cocaine to the public under a pizza with a special code. You can get your fix delivered to your door." "Wow, such an ingenious idea. You mean to tell me all 15 units know about the operation?" "No, no, slow down guys. The halfway house is the perfect cover for special trainees. They are trained before they hit the streets. Only certain employees are allowed to answer the order phone." "You mean to tell me they only take special orders?" "Come on guys, loads of regular customers call for pizza, but they know how to handle the specials. Let me explain, the code changes every two days to keep it real." Nicholas Smith is amused at the looks on both cops' faces, so he is working them. "Let me explain a typical call. The phone rings, 'GI Pizza #2, how can I help you?' 'I would like to place an order, 1 plain, 2 pepperonis with a side order of extra cheese.' '20 minutes, address please, on and on.' You get the address, walk in, pay for pizza, and sell as many bars as requested. Nice and clean, no one is suspicious. Just another pizza delivery man. In my case, I just got greedy. First things first, I need a transfer out to a safe house, or by tomorrow I am dead. No transfer, no more cooperation." Both Lieutenant Max and Detective Dean are totally blown away with this info and assure Mr. Smith that he would be transferred. They knock on the door and ask Sergeant Lisa to put Mr. Smith in a special isolated cell until further notice. They also instruct him, "No matter who inquiries about Smith's location, you are not to answer the question. You should call either Lieutenant Max or Detective Dean. Is that understood?" "Yes, sir." "You will receive a call with further instructions, do you understand?" "Yes, sir." "Put him in isolation pronto." Neither of them could leave the detention center fast enough to report to Captain Flynn. Both Lieutenant Max and Detective Dean are gasping for air after that session and decide to go see Captain Flynn together. Dean picks up the phone and calls him. Mary picks up the phone, as usual. "Mary, let me talk to the Captain." "He is on another call." "Go in and tell him it's urgent. I will hold for a minute." She quickly knocks on his door and delivers the message. The Captain answers, "What in hell is going on Dean?" "Captain, both Lieutenant Max and I are on our way. We have some big news! We should arrive in 15 minutes." Both of them can't drive fast enough. They finally arrive, pull up front, and rush out of the car. Even Sergeant Garcia could not finish his usual hellos as they rush by him down the hall and don't even knock on the door. In they go and into Captain Flynn's office. Mary looks lost, seeing the commotion as they pass her desk. Captain Flynn looks surprised at both of them. "Ok boys, slow down and take a seat." They explain their interview and all the information they received. The Captain is totally amazed, "What's next boys?" Dean speaks up, "Captain, we have this gift that was thrown in our lap. We have to move fast before we lose our witness." "What do you recommend? I can call the Mayor's office, explain the emergency, bring in Daren from the DEA, and come up with a fast plan." "I have something in mind, but please call the Mayor now." "Ok, Dean." Captain Flynn signals Mary, "She picks up the phone." "What can I do for you, Captain?" "Mary, call the Mayor and tell him that I need to talk to him, it's an emergency." "Ok, Captain." A few minutes go by, and the phone rings. "Captain, the Mayor's office is on line two." He picks up the phone. "What is the emergency, Captain?" "Mayor, we just got a major break in our case, and I need to fill you in fast." "Ok, I will be there in 15 minutes. I am on my way."

Lieutenant, I want you to stay in my office, contact Sergeant Lisa, and tell her to stand by. I will call him with instructions about Mr. Smith. It is very important that you stay in town with your witness at the detention center. The Mayor will make all the calls to cover you and the Sergeant." "Ok Dean, let's go." As he flashes by Mary's desk, she looks bewildered, and he blows her a kiss. Down the hall and out the door, he quickly gets in the Captain's car. The Captain looks at Dean, "Boy, Dean, you are really moving on this case, congrats!" "It's a team effort, Captain," he chuckles. "What's on your mind, Captain?" "I am sure word about Mr. Smith will be out quickly, so we don't have much time." "Captain, I am thinking let's wait before informing the Mayor." As they walk in through the door, they are escorted right into the Mayor's office, and he looks surprised and happy. "What's up, Captain?" "Mr. Mayor, let detective Dean explain the situation." Ok boys, sit down and take a breath."

Dean explains the interview at the detention center to the Mayor, and he is impressed. "What is next Dean?" "Mr. Mayor, I really don't think we have too much time, and I would recommend, of course with your permission, that you call Daren at the DEA and recommend he has an ambulance pick up Mr. Smith at the detention center under the cover that he attempted to commit suicide and bring him to a safe house until we decide the next step of the plan. To make it safe, the next day, we can put an article in the morning press that Mr. Smith was DOA at the hospital. That will give us a chance to catch our breath and continue our course and make the people behind Mr. Smith comfortable." "Dean, your mind works like a Hollywood scriptwriter's!" "I try, your honor." "Ok, let me call and meet with Daren, and I will call both of you within the hour. In the meantime, go back to Captain Flynn's office." They both felt a little relieved and headed back to the office. "Dean, that was one hell of an idea." "Thank you, sir."

Mentally exhausted, they reach the station, and as usual, a smiling Garcia gives them a big hello. The walk down the hall appears never-ending. Finally, they reach the Captain's office, and a big smile from Mary is just what the doctor ordered. Captain Flynn tells Lieutenant Max to come into his office. As soon as the door closes, Dean waves over to Mary and kisses her.

Twenty minutes later, Captain Flynn and Lieutenant Max stroll out. They look at Dean. "The plan is a go, just waiting for the Mayor to start the ball rolling." "Just sit and wait and have a cup of coffee."

"Captain, we need to have an emergency meeting to get this rolling without giving them the opportunity to get this witness killed in jail."

For the first time, the walk to Captain Flynn's office felt pleasant. As I open the door, Mary's smile was like a morning kiss. I had to stick to business. "Morning, Mary." "Hi, Dean. The boss should be ready in a few more minutes." As usual, his loud voice rang out, "Mary, is Dean here?" "Yes, Captain?" "Make sure Lieutenant Max is on his way." "Ok." "Come on in Dean." "Good morning." "Dean, nice presentation last week." "Thank your boss." "What's next? If it's ok, can we wait for Lieutenant Max?" No sooner I finish my sentence, Lieutenant Max walks in with an excited greeting, and the look on Flynn's face tells the story. So, Dean explains that the subject is well taken care of, and that Lieutenant Max has to call Sergeant Lisa to officially let them know at the detention center, he died of a heart attack. Flynn looks over at Lieutenant Max, "Take care of it as soon as we finish with the meeting." "Yes, sir." "That's the most important phase of this operation success. This way, all of his associates at the halfway house can feel less apprehensive, and the most important part of it is that Ms. Arleen realizes that we keep our word. Mr. Smith can then safely and without reservation tell us what we need to know. As soon as we complete our meeting, I will call Daren at the DEA so that he can proceed with our witness."

"Captain Flynn, for the record, my recommendation is that we keep this info to a very selective few. I personally think we should have Sergeant Scott put the heat on Grace so as to find out if any information is floating around about the pizza business. It seems that our friend Grace has not given us all the information to help us. After we set her up, let's put a little heat on her. It's time for her to earn her money. The newspaper part should be done within a few days, and then we can proceed with inspection and move once the coast is clear of any suspicion." "Good, let's keep the bus moving. By the way, Lieutenant, I want to thank you for your great cooperation and your knowledge of the detention center operation, and I don't want to forget the help provided by Sergeant Lisa and her team." "Thank you, brother." "In the past, did any member of your team have any contact with the company called GI importing company?" "Without anyone suspecting, I will go back and check previous weekly records." "Thanks, Lieutenant." After a brief pause, Captain Flynn says, "Ok, boys, get back to work and keep me informed." "Yes, sir." Slowly, I get up and wait until everyone has cleared the area. Making sure we are alone; I give Mary a kiss. I leave after waving goodbye and gesturing to her that I will call her. My phone rings, and

Scott's on the phone. "Dean, I need to talk to you." "Okay Scott. Come over tonight and bring some pizza. I will pay you." "You always say that, and I get stuck. You're the guy who never has any money." He starts to chuckle, "You know me well. See you tonight."

All day long, I just tried to see new angles and ideas that came to mind about the case. I kept reading my old notes, thinking maybe I forgot, misread, or overlooked something. The day seemed to fly by, and I was relieved that I had enough info for one day. I headed home and could not get into the house fast enough. It felt great to get in my T-shirt and shorts. I planted myself on my favorite chair. As soon as I close my eyes, the doorbell rings. It woke me up. I had to gather my senses. I open the door to see a smiling Scott. I must have been sleeping. I was reading this book for 10 minutes. "Stop and get your ass in here. By the way, how much do I owe you?" "My God! I'm going to have a heart attack. I can't believe you're paying this time! Hold on, let me recover from the shock." "How much?" "$14.00." Both of us started eating like we haven't had a meal in weeks, and all we did was an occasional grunt and kept on chewing. Finally, we both reached for the last piece, and Scotty was closer to the pie. As he reached out and snatched it up with a big smile, I just started laughing. After we finished, we looked at each other and started to laugh and laugh. "Let's get down to business," says Dean. "Let me know what's going on with our girl Grace." "Well, let's start with the Bolero Bar. It is under new management; the area is changing, and it needed new people." "What is Grace going to do? That was her hang out." Dean smiles, "The new people are Grace's old friends. You are not going to believe this. The new owner is Cooper." "What is that son of a bitch trying to do?" "He has been making a lot of money for a very long time and finally realized that it was the perfect cover for his drug business. Scott, this is a great country. You sell poison, get rich, and walk around." "Holy shit."

Dean, that's the job we chose." "Getting back to Grace, Cooper fired the entire staff, cleaned the place out, refurbished the bar, and renamed it 'The Bolero lounge.' Now it's a gay bar." It's a new world out there." You're lucky Dean that you found Mary. It gave you a new perspective on your life. Both of you are content and happy." "Just remember, Scott, you of all people knew me before I totally screwed up and was discontent and very unhappy." "I know, Dean. I feel good that you have finally turned the corner." "Thanks, Scott. Getting back to Grace…" Dean starts to laugh and gets louder. "What's so funny, Dean?" "Well, Grace has a new partner. His name is Paul, or should I say Phyllis." "What?" He continues to snicker. "What's so funny?" Scott is confused. "Well, remember when Grace got busted with her film company and we locked her and the entire crew? Paul was Phyllis then, and he was Grace's cellmate." "Oh my God! Life is strange, and you never know what's coming down the road. My mom always said that I should try to treat everyone nicely because you never know what's down the road." "Your mom was a smart lady. What the hell happened to you?" "What does Paul do for a living?" "He drives a truck for GI import's trucking company." Scott's laughter turns to panic. "Dean, what's wrong? You look like you saw a ghost. You're starting to look green. "Let me catch my breath." Scott is getting worried by the minute. "Boy I will kill that pizza shop owner. Looks like you have chest pain." "No, Scott. Let me catch my breath, and I will explain." "It better be good you son of a bitch. You just spoiled my dinner." It felt like a lifetime recovering from the shock. I took a deep breath and explained to Scott the complete background of the meeting with Smith, and he realized the magnitude of Grace's part in Cooper's organization. Both our minds started to go a mile a minute, wondering if Grace played everyone for a fool. Considering the complications of the situation, we spent half the night thinking about different scenarios. We both looked exhausted and wondered what to do, so I asked Scott to think back about Grace's actions, the places she visited, and any phone calls, etc., that he may have overheard. We both just started at the wall like two kids taking a test and did not know the answers. Finally, Scott started to piece back her activities, daily bar orders, interactions with customers, etc., but nothing seemed unusual. However, she and Paul seemed to develop a taste for pizza. They ordered twice in a week. "That piece of crap! She has been playing us all along." He told me, "Never trust a snake." Scott had a faraway look on his face and looked lost. I calmed him down and explained to him the past meeting with the Mayor, DEA, and all the parties involved. Both of us took a large, deep breath and tried to compose ourselves. We just sat without saying a word to each other and just looked into space. "What a night."

I finally realized that we were still in the game and explained to Scott to put all his efforts into Grace's activities and our boy Cooper. The more I think about it, everything is okay. We just have to be more careful with Grace and put our eyes on Paul and his stops. "Oh my God! It's 6:30 in the morning. Scott, you might as well clean up and have breakfast here and go to work." "Ok. Listen, Dean, let's not have pizza here for a while." Both of us started to laugh. "I'm going to take a nap before I go to work." "Use the couch in the living room. I'm going to bed myself, goodnight."

CHAPTER 10

No matter how hard I tried to forget, sleeping seemed impossible. All I wanted to do was reevaluate the situation. Finally, it dawned on me. Cooper's long and lucrative life on the street lasted long because he always made sure he covered his bases if he had any doubts or suspicion about anyone working for him, and then he realized that it was a brilliant move on his part. I did not realize that my father's shadow was still around me in one way or another. The old man still has his hand on my future. "Pop, you're gone but not forgotten." "I'm starting to feel better about the situation and realize that we're dealing with a very smart organization and that we must look beyond the average approach. As soon as I get to work, I will schedule a meeting with my boss and explain my latest finding. Life is good, keep your wits about you and use your brains.

Make sure that the plan is moving as laid out, and check with Lieutenant Max how the release of the news article is progressing. That's the key. Boy, talking to yourself is not bad; a psychiatrist would probably put me on more medications, but at least I come up with good answers. Boy, you really are arrogant.

This is really going to be an interesting day. I can't wait to get started! While driving to work, I'm trying to think of how to approach the boss and still keep his attitude positive about the situation. But here comes the old man in my head. I did not realize the influence he had on me until just a few hours ago. "Pop, sorry I never told you how much I loved you while you were around, but I guess you were always with me in spirit."

As I slowly drive to work today, my mind is going a mile a minute, trying to figure out what my next move is going to be. I have to just be myself and constantly use my brain to continue to visualize all possibilities, look at all the areas, and just move with the circumstances. I finally get to the station, and Sergeant Garcia's smiling face greets me with his usual, "Good morning, Detective Dean." "Good morning, Sergeant." I walk across the hall and get to Captain Flynn's office. Mary looks surprised at me, "Morning, good looking. What a pleasant surprise! What's going on? I haven't seen you in a few days." "I guess I forgot how to use the phone, so I came to see you and to talk to the boss. Is he available?" "He will be in a little late today, in 1/2 hour or so." "Great." Mary gets up slowly, and my eyes are glued to this beautiful lady. "Give me 10 minutes, and I will make us coffee." "Thank you." But first, I walked over and gave her a kiss. "What's that for?" "No reason. You're just so beautiful, and I just wanted to thank you." "Boy, you have come a long way from the jerk I met a long time ago." "Thank you, but you weren't the main motivation factor behind my change." She smiled and walked away. "Thank you for coffee." Within a few minutes, Mary comes back with coffee. It tastes great.

The conversation continues, and it feels like communicating with someone special in your life. But just when things start to get interesting, the boss walks in with a surprised look on his face. "Dean, I was going to ask Mary to call you. You saved me some time. Give me five minutes and come into my office. Mary, please give me a cup of coffee, as usual." Playing second fiddle to Detective Dean, Mary smiles falsely. The Captain clears his throat, looks over, and signals me to get in his office. I promptly take the hint and sit down. Within a few minutes, Mary comes to the door and brings in his coffee.

"First things first, Detective Dean, as you probably know Lieutenant Max has made the Captain's list at least five times, but there have been no openings or promotions. However, a Captain from his precinct just informed me that he will retire within a few months. Finally, I think Lieutenant Max will be promoted. I will recommend Lieutenant Max to the chief, and he will add his name to the list, along with other candidates. First, I will personally tell Lieutenant Max about the recommendation to keep this mouth shut until its official." "That's great news! Lieutenant Max is a professional policeman and a good, respected person. I'm sure he's going to be overwhelmed by the news." "Ok Dean." I explained to the Captain my meeting with Sergeant Scott last night. He gave it some thought, approached the situation quietly, hesitated for a few minutes, and said, "Make sure you keep me informed if anything changes." I explain to him that Cooper's a very cautious professional who makes sure he has someone in his pocket to keep him informed of any doubts about anyone working for him. "When you think about it, boss, I have my doubts about Grace. She gets busted and within a few months she has an opportunity to get out on bail. As I explained to Sergeant Scott, our number one priority is Grace. He knows this 100%. Please ask Daren if he has any update on the local newspaper articles on Mr. Smith, "Sure, Dean. By the way, keep all this information between us." "Yes, sir." "I will call you after I speak to Daren." "Thank you, boss"

On his way out, Dean sees Mary and says, "See you later, beautiful." He is happy and a little apprehensive. It's a mixed bag of emotions going through his mind. He needs to end this case right.

Days go by, and Dean finally feels a bit better about the case. One morning, Lieutenant Max calls to inform him of a newspaper article appearing in the local paper. He lets out a small sigh of relief, if only for the moment. It seems like the week is flying by, and I have to start to slow down and let things happen. I cannot push too hard and risk screwing things up, but that's easier said than done. I'm looking forward to the weekend with Mary, and that should settle me down. After a great weekend of total relaxation and trying to just become a normal person, reality caught up with me. I received a phone call from Captain Flynn asking me to come for a meeting with Lieutenant Max about a Double D inspection, and he told me not to be late. Who is Double D? Captain Flynn chuckles at the question and responds, "I tried to make a funny, Daren from the DEA." Now I get it. "You have no sense of humor" He shakes his head and walks away dialing Sargent Scott to get an update. The phone rings, and there is no answer, so he leaves a message. He's starting to get antsy on what to do. I should just concentrate on the things I can control and keep working on the phone. Scott calls back, "What's up?" "I wonder if there's been any movement with our local truck driver." "The only thing I can provide is a complete list of every pizza shop in the area that is serviced by GI Imports." I kept my distance and took photos to document the stores. I can't believe that it's such a large operation with the availability to push so much product, and no one had a hint of what's really going on, American ingenuity at its best. The more you look into our boy Cooper, the more you really have to respect the professional operation he runs. Not only is he a pretty boy but also a very smart operator with no second thoughts about getting away at any cost. He takes no chance. "Scott, you're dealing with a complete pro, so you better be extremely careful in your movements around him and his people. He is making money from prostitution and drugs but keeps a low profile to avoid making noise."

"I don't want to tell you what's at stake. We have to be able to get to Cooper's locations, but it must be a different operation how goods are being handled. I'm puzzled about that. I have to talk to Daren to press Mr. Smith for any information on this operation. Even a rumor or hunch will be helpful, Scott."

"Start walking to the pizza shops. This will help me get

an idea of the whole operation. It's too big to be a one-man operation. It's quiet and efficient. Good luck." Time seems to move slowly. You bet that's the only thing on my mind, which is going a mile a minute. I have to learn to relax, but who am I kidding? It's my nature. Things are getting crazy around here. I'm starting to talk to myself. I need to talk to Mary to bring me back to reality. I need some sleep before I pass out standing. As the morning light shines in my room with all its glory it reminds me to get out of bed and get moving. I have a meeting with the DEA and was told not to be late. I have to meet him at 10 o'clock. Throughout the drive, I panic in my car. I walk into the station up to the door. Things seem so different. Sergeant Garcia is not there at the front desk to greet me with his smiling face. I walk down to Captain Flynn's. Seeing Mary puts me in a good mood. I can smell her perfume. "Good morning, beautiful." I give her a kiss and walk into the other room. Captain Flynn says, "Good morning, gentlemen. How are you doing Daren?" "Living the dream." We both smile. "Relax, Mary is bringing us coffee. After the coffee arrives, Captain Flynn remarks, "Help yourselves, and let's get this meeting moving." As he looks my way and asks me to explain the current situation, I give my presentation. I can see the look of concern on their faces. I continue explaining the approach we are taking to stay on top of the situation. Daren explains that the death of our witness, Mr. Smith, was published about two weeks ago and did not stir any question in the community? But he also made it a point to keep a strong eye on Mr. Cooper's operation by making sure that Scott spends more time with our girl, Grace." "Yes, sir. "Captain, did you also explain Lieutenant Max about his potential promotion?" "Yes, and the Lieutenant got a little emotional when I broke the news. It was kind of nice to see that hard ass look vulnerable." Captain Flynn asked more questions, and he specifically asked Daren about how the investigation with Mr. Smith was coming along. I explain, "He felt relieved about the preparations taken to keep him invisible, and he has a tendency to not just talk about it. He seems to answer any question we asked him with no problem, but I feel he will eventually just start to talk at length. We are pleased because we have checked his info, and he has been 100% on target. He explained that our boy Cooper is the main controlling boss in that area. We continued asking him about the drug supplies, and he seemed kind of unsure and really has not opened up about it. But we were able to find out the complete operation going on in the halfway house and about the Board members. So far, the attorney sitting on the board is the person in charge. We are still trying to find out if he is connected to GI imports. I feel Mr. Smith will continue to speak more freely now that he is invisible. As usual, our meetings will be kept on a need-to-know basis for now, and at the proper moment, I will advise the other members." "Ok, Dean, I understand. Stay in touch and have a good day." As we slowly get up and walk out, I made sure that I was the last one to leave so I could spend some time with Mary. I gave her a hug and a kiss and motioned that I would call her. She smiled and nodded. As I walked out of the building, I heard a familiar voice, "How are you detective?" "You are a lucky man." I just smiled. As I was on my way thinking of my next move, my phone rings Detective Dean I see you in the parking lot. "Hold on, I want to speak to you." "Ok." So, a few minutes go by, and Daren gets in my car. "What's up, Dean? In your presentation, you hit a nerve explaining Grace's new partner." I give him a detailed picture of the situation, and he is very quiet for a few minutes. "Dean, I think the key to this operation's movement is the GI import driver. I will assign an agent to that truck. Track his every move, and I will be in contact with you." "Thank you, Sir. "Have a great day."

CHAPTER 11

TIME GOES BY DAY BY DAY, WITH NO RESULTS OR NEW LEADS. IT'S very frustrating. It seems you're working on several things at a time. Keep pushing. It's easy to think about motivation but very difficult to implement. Sleeping, eating, thinking about something that I have perhaps overlooked. Look forward to a good night's sleep, hoping the next day is going to be better. Finally, my phone rings. It's Scott on the other line with excitement in his voice. "What's going on Scott?" "Dean, I have been keeping a very close eye on Grace, and it seems on Monday, Cooper made his usual visit to the Bolero. Dean, I am becoming a regular barfly. I even have my own stool." "This doesn't sound good. Stop the bullshit and get to the point." "You must be having a hard week." "Not really, just frustrated." "Ok, maybe this will put a little spark in your week. On Monday night, Cooper made his usual visit, and he seemed very unhappy with Grace. He pointed his finger and raised his voice. He ripped her a new one and from her reaction, she didn't seem concerned. When her partner came in and Grace started giving Phil the info, it must have been very personal because he was mad as hell and started yelling at Grace. I tried to provide her with some support, but she told me to fuck off and to mind my own business. After a few minutes, she came back and apologized to me. Just before closing time, Cooper came and started yelling at her again. This time, it became loud and ugly. Both of them screamed at each other, and Cooper told her that he is her boss and that she should just shut up and listen to him. Grace gave him the finger, and that really infuriated Cooper. He slapped her across the face, knocking her back. The look on her face was very unusual." "You asshole." "I was just following your instructions to really keep an eye on both of them." "Scott, I think it's starting to come apart." "He turned around and walked out telling her to get her shit together, you know. Grace gave him the finger again and started to drink. A bartender with a big mouth shouldn't drink with customers. "Scott, keep the pressure. Maybe it's the crack we were looking for." After the excitement was over, it was time to make a pit stop, the Bolero Lounge. One of the employees in the room looks at me and remarks, "It's like a rerun. Every time the boss shows up, it doesn't seem to affect Grace. She looks like she's in a trance and that really pisses Cooper off."

"Let's face it, Dean, the boss thinks she's on perpetual vacations. She's done nothing since we took her under our wing, no results, no leads, nothing. I think it will be helpful if you talk to her Dean and remind our girl of her obligation." "I have to be very careful in the way I contact her. Before I forget, Dean, her partner picks her up after work." "I will call her tomorrow; in the meantime, keep up your good work and be careful." "Let's face it. She has a job, a roof over her head, and money in her pocket. She does not need us. I have to bring her back to reality. The sooner the better." I will talk to her soon."

I asked Grace to contact me. It's been two days, and I've heard nothing from her. I'm starting to get worried waiting for her to call. If I have to, I will have the courts contact her. I hope it does not come to that."

Finally, after a few anxious days, I spoke to Grace. She agreed to meet face-to-face. I told her the location, and she was comfortable coming there. The next day, the meeting took place. Initially, she was a little cold, but slowly, the tension dropped. She looked older and tired, but with the same fire in her personality. After the niceties were over, I reminded her of the commitment they made, and she started to feel more at ease. She told me about her new partner. They had been connected back since her days in the adult movie company. He was a director. We both chuckled, and our situation became more intense, as she told me that they both served in jail together. She said, "Dean, as you already are aware, he moved in with me, and it seemed to go well. For the first time, I was really at ease. I started drinking again, and in one of my stupors, I confided in him about Cooper's girlfriend, Paige. It was a fiasco. Nothing seemed wrong until we had that conversation. He told me that Cooper's lawyer got him a job with GI imports. After that, Cooper seemed to come around the bar more often, and I started to wonder if Phil had spilled our conversation to Cooper. It really made me wonder about his sudden interest in that conversation he asked about that night again and I told him I didn't know what he was talking about. He became angry, and we started to scream at each other. As Cooper's visits became more frequent, I started to become more concerned, hoping Phil did not give out my secret." "It all seems concerning. He is the master of manipulation, and we are very well aware of her gift. I tried to make her feel that I believed her, but deep down inside, she is trying to give us a false impression to get us on her case. She has always been manipulative. She continued, "Back then, in my previous state of mind, I was a victim. I tried to inform old Phil." She explained that he drives the GI import truck. I tried to push her, but she became a little vague and seemed to stop talking. We parted company. I reminded her of her responsibility. We left the area as discreetly as possible. I finally realized that Grace had been playing us all along. I have to meet Captain Flynn and explain to him this Grace situation. I still feel that Phil has sold out Grace to Cooper, and he is just waiting to move on her. I will call Sergeant Scott to get his point of view, but in my gut, I always felt that the whole operation was going smoothly.

Sergeant Scott told me that the Bolero was looking for a second-shift bartender. I will contact Daren at the DEA. It may be the perfect spot for an agent. That way, we will have more eyes and ears in the bar. Let's see how he feels about it. As soon as I reach home, I'm going to change and start jogging again. That was the only thing that made me less stressful. After completing my 2 miles and a little more, I was relieved. I acquired a new feeling, it's called "tired and aching." I showered and made myself a quick meal. My phone rang, and Sergeant Scott started to inform me that Cooper's sports car was stolen, and he reported it to the police. "I can't believe that." "Cooper's car getting stolen does not make any sense to me." "Scott, stranger things have happened. Keep in touch."

I needed to change my approach in this case, so I started digging for information on the attorney involved with the local halfway house board, and the same attorney serves on a board in the Jacksonville area. It all makes sense, since the bail bond company is from Jacksonville. It proves how well-organized the operation is. Two days of digging, and I got nothing that jumps out about a young attorney trying to establish his future on the surface but a person of intense interest. I get a second call from Scott in the last few days, and I asked Scott what's going on. He informs me, "He started to tail Phil, and it was all very routine until he observed his daily deliveries. He picked up a second guy, who he did not even give a second thought. The helper worked with Phil, all very normal. About two hours into the delivery, on the way to the next one, this guy was the prototype. I stayed on him. In a car, he picked up the helper, and when he took his hat off to get in the car, I noticed it was Cooper. I was not ready for that move, and I was startled. It took me a few minutes to get back to my senses and could not wait to call you." "Scott, stay closer to Grace than ever." "Ok, Dean." "I dialed Captain Flynn's office and asked Mary for the first possible time for a visit. She told me to wait, and in a few minutes, she came back to tell me he was available Wednesday at 11:00 o'clock. Mary remarked, "Dean, are you Ok?" "Sorry beautiful. But it's important that I see him as soon as possible." "Mary, after Wednesday's meeting, are you available for an early dinner?" "Dean, I will always be available for you." "Thank you beautiful."

As I got off the phone, my mind started to think about all the different scenarios possible, and none of them had a good ending. I could not believe that I was looking forward to continuing with my jogging, and it was the only part of the day that kept my sanity at an even keel.

Deep down, I had a bad feeling. Grace is in deep trouble, and she is starting to feel the pressure, knowing she can talk her way out of it. I can't mention to Cooper her revelation, her relationship with his old girlfriend Paige. He will quickly figure out that she has made it deal to get out. I feel he never believed her story, but he did not have any proof; otherwise, until his contact with Phil, and that's a position Cooper would not tolerate. His insecurity of not having total control will get to her. The next day cannot come quickly enough. I was tired and frustrated, and sleep was my only peace. Early the next day, I called Lieutenant Max and tried to pick up his brain about the situations that transpired during the weekly detectives' meeting, he told me everything was as usual: DUI's, bar fights, etc. I asked if anyone had any info on Cooper's stolen car. He chuckled, "Not really." "Thanks, Lieutenant." I stopped for a quick cup of coffee and continued trying to come up with other ideas. I started to continue further research on the halfway house attorney, hoping to find something that could help us. But I came up dry. I contacted some of my street informants and found nothing of interest. Scott gave me a quick call to inform me that Phil came in the bar and told the management that Grace was sick and needed a few days off. As he walked by, he winked his eye. He said it's a combination of their anniversary together and that they needed some time to party and calm Grace down. "I had this awful feeling in my stomach, like the one when my dad passed away." "Scott, forget about anything you had planned. Stay with the love birds and keep your eye on their every move."

No sooner I got off the phone with Scott, Captain Flynn calls me to pick him up at 11:30 tomorrow outside of the front door. "Dean, I need to get out of the office. The last few days have been hell, and I need a break." "Ok, boss." "And don't be late." "Yes sir." I headed back to my house, got something to eat, grabbed a beer, and started doing some research on my computer. That's the last I remember. I opened my eyes, and I had a warm beer in front of me, and it was 4:00 o'clock in the morning. I could not stop laughing, so I decided that it's time to go upstairs—something I haven't been able to do for a very long time. I still could not stop laughing. Man, I must be getting old. I haven't laughed this much in a very long time, and it's a strange calmness that I never experienced before. I do not know how to handle it—very strange! I felt like a 10-year-old with no problems looking for my next ice cream cone, and boy, that's a good feeling.

The next morning, as I started to drive to meet Captain Flynn, something changed in me. I did not want to wake up from this dream. Whether it was real or not, I kept on smiling and driving. I waited for Captain Flynn to arrive, and finally, his usual gruff voice brought me back to reality. Captain Flynn remarked, "What the hell are you smiling about?" "Oh, nothing inspector." "Ok, Dean. Where are we going for lunch?" "I figure we go to Gavin's deli." "Good choice. I was in the mood for a good Cuban sandwich." There wasn't too much small talk on the way. We finally arrived and got seated in a few minutes. The waiter took our order. I started to explain the present situation, and he looked a little nervous and remarked, "Dean, this luncheon was supposed to keep me calm." Both of us smiled, and I explained the steps that we had taken. He did not make any other remarks and only spoke about local sports. Both of us tried to enjoy lunch. The food was great, and the conversation felt like it was scripted, but nevertheless, you are never completely at ease when having lunch with your boss. I paid the bill, and Captain Flynn left the tip. Not too much small talk on the way over to the police station as well, and as we arrived, he gave his usual instructions, "Keep in touch." "Will do, boss." As the pressure of the case mounted, it crept back into my system; well, it tried. My mind felt refreshed, and I started to pursue new leads and ideas. The rest of the time seemed to fly by. For the rest of the week, I just continued to dig and hope that something would provide good leads. The highlight was having dinner with Mary, just trying to be a normal guy, and having an enjoyable date with my girlfriend.

CHAPTER 12

TUESDAY MORNING, MY PHONE RINGS, AND SCOTT SEEMED RATTLED. "What's going on, Scott?" "For the past few days, there's been no sign of our favorite couple, Phil and Grace. I stayed with them throughout, just leaving every few hours, taking care of my personal needs and coming back. A pizza truck made a delivery on Sunday night, the usual activity. The only thing is that I have seen little movement from our couple. I am going to drop in at the Bolero tonight and just check out Grace's attendance. I will call you later." "Don't worry about the time, just call me whenever possible." "Ok." "This situation is starting to bother me now. I'm going to be on pins and needles until you call." "Wait for my call, Dean". "Ok." I just can't believe that our lawyer friend from the halfway house, Mr. Chris Flag, has such a limited background. I just have a gut feeling that I just have to start digging into the Jacksonville area code. After a few hours of computer work, something finally comes up. One of the attorneys who represents GI imports is also one of the two attorneys who represents Jake's bond service. Now, everything is starting to make sense.

Scott finally called around 3:00 o'clock in the morning and tells me that Grace has not shown up at work in two days. That's not Grace. She would go to work, no matter how sick she felt and would get just drunk to feel better. "Scott, tomorrow, make it a point to go over to her apartment and check it out. Don't leave until you get some answers. One way or another, you get my drift?" "Loud and clear, Dean." I finally fell asleep. As usual, I open my eyes, slumped back in front of my second-best friend, the laptop, at 6:00 o'clock in the morning. Things are slowly becoming normal again, and I have to shut down and go upstairs to bed. Well, I might as well take advantage of hard work. I started out on the couch, and it feels good. I opened my eyes, and it's 4:00 o'clock in the afternoon. That's one hell of a nap. I got up and made myself a sandwich. No sooner did I start to enjoy it, the phone rang, and it was Scott. "What's going on, buddy?" There was no answer, so I had to ask again, "Scott, what's going on?" It's not like Scott to be at a loss for words. Now, I am really starting to worry. "Goddammit Scott! What's happening?" For as long as we have known each other, I did not expect this emotional situation. "Spill it out, man. You are a well-trained police officer!" "I know, Dean, but it really got too close to my suspects. I slowly opened the door, and Phil and Grace were sprawled out. Grace on the crappy couch and Phil on the floor next to her. My first impression was that they both must be passed out drunk. Something did not feel right—no movement, nothing. I took a chance and checked both their pulses. I felt nothing." "Are you kidding me?" "I wish I was, Dean. I carefully started looking around the area. A white residue was still on the tabletop. A large pizza box was lying open with a few slices on the floor." "Scott, get the hell out of their apartment as quick as possible, wait a few hours, pick the most isolated area you can find, make an anonymous call to the police, and come over my house. Let's talk about the situation. Lieutenant Max does not know that you have been involved with the group, and I want to keep it that way for the time being."

My mind was going a mile a minute, and I could not wait to speak to Scott. Around 11:00 o'clock, finally a knock at the kitchen door, and Scott walks in. I had a cold beer in my hand, and he guzzled it down in record time. We walked into the kitchen, and he walked over to the fridge and grabbed another. "Now you're the Scott I grew up with". "Sorry, Dean. For a moment, I lost it. I don't ever forget that just because we carry a badge, it does not mean that we lose our compassion, and this feeling is something I have not experienced in a very long time. It's called humanity." "Sit your ass down and explain yourself a little." "There's not much to explain. They looked like just another couple facing their demons, and they paid the price. The difference is that we both know where it came from, and it was a very professional move on their part. In my opinion, Phil revealed to Cooper what Grace had told him, and our boy Cooper figured the only way to keep it clear was to make it look like just another overdose, nothing special." "How did you handle the phone call?" "I waited until I was it was dark and carefully got out of the apartment. Once I was out of the area, I took the 395 out of town. What's my approach going to be tomorrow?" "Just go about your normal routine, visit the Bolero tomorrow and keep your eyes open. I will be in touch." "Look, Scott, stay over tonight and then and try to relax. There's plenty of cold cuts in the fridge. Make yourself a sandwich, and goodnight." The alarm woke me up. I got out of bed, showered, dressed, and went downstairs for a cup of coffee. Scott was already gone. I continued with my usual routine, and my phone started ringing. I was Captain Flynn, "Dean, get to my office as soon as possible." "Ok, boss." I just had to act very calm when he broke the news that I already knew of. No sooner I hang up the phone, Lieutenant Max calls. "Hello, Max. How are you?" "Get your ass in here ASAP for a meeting." "Thanks for the call, but Captain Flynn just called me." As I reached the station, I had to keep my composure and look concerned. I think I can do that; I hope. Finally, I arrived and walked as fast as possible to Captain Flynn's office. Lieutenant Max was already in the room, waiting with a concerned look on his face. "Good morning, Lieutenant." "What's going on, Captain Flynn?" He opens the door. "Pour yourselves a cup of coffee. I will be with you guys shortly." "Ok, Captain." His door opens, and he calls us in. He looked very somber, and I tried to emulate his attitude.

"Ok, Lieutenant Max, give us the latest report." "Gentlemen, last night, we received an anonymous call. A potential overdose: nothing seemed out of the ordinary, and the detective on duty followed the call to a house on Flagler St. After a few knocks on the door that they identified, there was no response. They force themselves through the door. In the living room, they observed two lifeless individuals. They checked for pulses; both were dead. They immediately called for the coroners; they arrived shortly. No explanation needed. It was all very routine. The bodies were removed, and the investigation began. The search for any potential clues, etc., was on, but to the experienced eye, it seemed like another overdose, something they had experienced way too often. They continued to look around for identification; it was found on the female, her name is Grace Pastore, and the man was identified as Phil Granda." It all seemed routine until Lieutenant Max was informed of their names, and he realized that other people were part of the ongoing investigation. He immediately contacted Captain Flynn. I informed both of them of the ongoing shadow program I developed after Miss Pastore started to give vital information to the DEA and also informed them about Sergeant Scott and his daily routine program. I also explained to both of them the previous information that Sergeant Scott was able to provide. They both seemed a little agitated, and I just explained that no disrespect was intended. I also explained that we have proof about Cooper's involvement. Captain Flynn finally gave me a forced smile, "You sneaky bastard!" "Just doing my job, sir."

"I will contact the Mayor and inform him about this situation. Lieutenant Max, thank you for the good work and for bringing this to our attention. Keep an eye on the results of the toxicology report, but don't attract any attention to it. Have a good day, Lieutenant, and keep me in the loop." "Thank you, sir."

"Dean, stand by until I contact the Mayor." As soon as Lieutenant Max closed the door, Captain Flynn remarks, "Now give me the real story." I explained to him what Scott and I had to do to make the crime scene look like a normal tragedy. He gave me a half smile and remarked, "You have a lot of your dad's mindset." Mary opens the door and is surprised to see us. "Good morning. Did I miss anything?" "Oh no, it was just an emergency. Mary, as soon as you get settled, call Dana at the Mayor's office and tell her that I need to speak to him on an urgent matter quickly." "Yes sir." She turned toward me and gave me a wink. We both just continued to nervously drink our coffee, and Mary comes back in the room and informs us that he has an appointment with the Mayor at 9:30 that morning.

"Dean, both of us will meet the Mayor, and you will explain him the complete picture. Don't leave anything out. Tell him about the entire approach and just let him catch his breath. I am sure he will be lost and will ask for suggestions. Don't give him any bullshit, just massage his ego. Do what you do best, explain your approach, and let him, as usual, get involved. His mind will be trying to figure out how this case can help him in his reelection program. Just stay positive." I wanted to smile, but for once I was smart and just looked at the floor. "Ok, Dean, let's get moving." We walked down the hall and slowly left the building. We took our time, and during the ride to the Mayor's office, not a word was spoken. Strange but nice.

We finally arrive and walk up to the door. As usual, we are greeted by Dana. "Good morning, gents. I will inform the Mayor that you are here." It was a little unusual that the Mayor came out of his office and walked us in. "Dana brings us some coffee please. Sit down. Let's wait a few minutes." Dana arrives, and I could tell that the Mayor was a little nervous and did not want her to hear any part of this meeting. "Dana, please hold off any calls until I call you." "Ok, Mr. Mayor." "Ok guys, you called this meeting emergency meeting." Captain Flynn looked at me, "Detective Dean will bring you up to date." I started to give him the whole picture from the very beginning slowly and carefully to make sure I did not overload him with too much information, and I paused to make sure he was absorbing the complete scheme without him feeling lost. At one point, he asked me to take a breath and just let him absorb all of the information I had shared. I specifically reminded him of our last meeting, Cooper's connection with the dead DEA agent, and the suspicious warehouse fires on the waterfront. It all seemed to finally hit home. "Now, I am starting to see the whole picture," he remarks. As I continue to bring him up to speed about the present drug overdose situation, he suddenly became very loud. "I am not going to let him get away with this." Both Captain Flynn and I just looked at each other. Campaign reelection ideas just hit the Mayor. You could feel he was excited and that his mind was going a mile a minute. He started asking, "What we are going to do?" Captain Flynn looked at me and remarked, "Thank you Detective Dean. I will continue." He took a deep breath and explained to the Mayor, "We must act with caution and think about the proper approach. We have to involve the DEA for their expertise and also plan the FBI's involvement without any making any ordinary moves that could give us away. I can assure you, your honor, there are enough people on the street looking and listening to anything different happening. If I might, your honor, I would like to meet with Daren on a fishing day trip, give him the complete layout, and get his ideas. Let's just not push this opportunity and let's just get it right." "Captain, that is one hell of an ingenious operation on our noses." "Mr. Mayor, we are not dealing with a local small dealer; we must plan out completely, have every detail planned out, and only share it with the people involved. I will get started on planning the operation, and when we feel ready to move, we will inform you directly." "Ok, guys, you may feel like I am studying for a college final and hoping for a good grade." "Thank you, Mr. Mayor, I will be in touch." As we leave the office and thank Dana, we both just look at each other, and Captain Flynn nods to me to just stay quiet. The walk to the car was longer than the arrival. "What did I tell you about his reelection mindset?" "Yes sir." "Our meeting stays between us." "Yes sir." "I will start to move this plan in all dimensions, start calling me on a daily basis around 2:00 o'clock every day until further notice. Drop me at the office and take the rest of the day off. Take some rest because you're going to need it. I will be in touch." "Yes sir." It was very difficult to think about what had just happened, so, as usual, I started using my imagination and planning my approach. It was enough to give me a headache. Thinking about it, the list of stories that Sergeant Scott gave me involved only one side at the present time, and we couldn't take any chances with the rest of them. I am starting to get a migraine headache. Please let me find my aspirin. I decided to call Sergeant Scott and asked about any changes at the bar. He told me that it was the same as usual, but the local police visited the bar and asked the staff questions about Grace and Phil. Everyone was puzzled about the police asking so many questions. Finally, they explained that they were both found in their apartment with an apparent overdose. They continued to ask questions, and as usual, the staff narrated their own versions. As I listened to them, my mind knew the real truth, and it was hard to just sit among them. But it did not seem to affect the crowd. They just continued to dance and enjoy themselves. They had no idea of the tragedy. I asked Scott to be very careful; he was in the deep. He said he'll watch his every move. After I hung up, reality made me think about what all of us go through every day. I just felt tired, stressed out, and empty. My body was beat up. Early to bed was my only reward so off to bed I went.

CHAPTER 13

IT SEEMED LIKE I JUST CLOSED MY EYES, AND MY MORNING ALARM shook through my bedroom. I slowly got up and started my usual routine. At least I was home. How exciting can breakfast be? I try to make the best of the situation until my 2:00 o'clock call with the boss. It was a slow, comfortable, lazy day; somehow, I couldn't remember the last time it happened, but I really felt great in my own way. I just enjoyed it. Around 10:00 o'clock, I called Mary and asked her to meet me for an early dinner. She asked me to pick her up around 7:00 o'clock, and this time, she was going to pick the destination. I told her, "You're the boss." She laughed and said, "You learn fast. The best thing to do is to keep your mouth shut." At two o'clock, per instructions, I called the boss, and he filed me in on the progress, covering all the parties involved. I did not realize the efficiency of Captain Flynn until now. He informed me of the Saturday fishing trip, not my favorite, but I just kept my mouth shut and agreed. He told me about the time and place and, as usual, asked me not to be late. "I know you hate fishing, Dean." "Yes sir, I will be there with my seasickness pills, ready to listen, learn, and just laugh." Now I really understand what it's like to work from home: nice, but confining; not bad, but not my cup of tea. I started to look over my notes, trying to make sure I do not forget any situation or detail that might be important for my meeting. No matter how small it might be, in my opinion, it was important. As I sit home alone with my ideas, contemplating all different angles and moves, it all brings me back to the realization that I have a lot to be thankful for. Above all, my calming force, Mary, and all the people who helped me out here. I don't mean to get melancholy, but maybe it's the calm before the storm that's making me nervous. Wow! It's hard trying to stay normal. My self-evaluated psychology moment! I better make a move and get ready for my date with Mary. I got dressed and picked up Mary, and we both had a wonderful dinner and a romantic evening. The hell with a psychiatrist! A date with Mary is all I need to get my engine moving and have a new outlook on my assignment. Boy, love is great!

Saturday could not come soon enough. Although I had tried fishing before, I was ready with my pills. I made sure not to eat breakfast so as to keep me a little safer. Off we go chugging along to his favorite fishing hole! It seemed like an eternity, but it was my sea legs talking to me. We finally dropped the anchor. We were there for a day of fishing, and for that long, we could always fake it. We put suntan lotion on our faces. Boy, great acting on our part. Once we're settled, Captain Flynn starts off with his approach. Daren attentively listens and then asks Flynn to let him absorb the information. He then gives his opinion. It was a good pause for all of us, and it gave everyone a moment to think and evaluate the situation and give our opinions. Daren came out with a different idea, which made more sense, and after Flynn thought about it and agreed with him, they both looked at me. I just went along with it and gave my input on how to handle the employees once we nab them. They had a surprised look on their faces, and they both gave me the thumbs-up. That was a response I never expected. They continued discussing different scenarios, but the previously agreed-upon scenario was finalized. I felt my face burning, and I know we all lost track of time. It was not right that my sunburn was used as a timer; they both started laughing. "Ok, boys, let's pull up the anchor and get home. We looked at each other, and Daren remarked, "Boys, you really have to put bait on your line to catch fish." "Shut up smarty," says Captain Flynn, and we all smile. The dock could not come quickly enough. We bid each other our usual goodbyes, and Captain Flynn said, "Dean, call me tomorrow." I cannot get home fast enough to shower and finally get something to eat. Fishing sucks! I made myself a very nice dinner and ate it like it was my last meal before going to the electric chair. It was great to stop rocking and rolling. When I got into the living room, I just sat there and tried to relax. The next thing I remember, it was 4:30 in the morning. What and the heck has become of my life? The couch felt like an old friend, so I just closed my eyes and tried to go to sleep. The phone rang. I looked up, and it was 11 o'clock. I could not believe I had slept that long. I answered, and it was Lieutenant Max. "Good morning, Dean. How are you doing?" "Lieutenant, I wanted to give you an update on the toxicology report of our couple. It was almost 60% fentanyl, impossible to survive once ingested; it was a very high dosage." "Thank you, Dean, for the update." I just sat and realized that whoever was involved knew exactly what they had to do, and Phil was caught in the process, thinking he was going to survive. It's 2:00 o'clock, and I have to make my usual phone call to the boss. After the usual salutations, he opened with the toxicology report. "Yes sir. Lieutenant Max made me aware of it." "By the way, Dean, our next meeting will be on Thursday, and it's golf this time. Do you play golf?" "No sir." "Ok. Pick me up at around 8:00 o'clock at the usual place, and I will give you the directions. We are going to play at the Mayor's private club. Just tag along, and listen, be prepared. Carry some suntan lotion. At least this time you will not be sick." "Fear I may be just bored. Thank you, sir. I can't wait.". "By the way, they will serve breakfast. "I will explain to the Mayor our operation." "I could do all the explaining to the Mayor, Chief of Police, and all the other members involved. "Thank you, sir." "And as usual, don't be late. Have a good day, Dean." "Thank you, sir."

As soon as I hung up, I tried to give myself a little background knowledge about golf. Well, at least it was a change of pace. The more I researched, the more confused I became. I tried to look for any kind of tournaments on TV so that I don't look stupid and confused. Good luck with that, but I'm sure I'm going to try. Finally, the big day arrived, and I was looking forward to the game. I drove to the station, waited for Captain Flynn to meet me in the parking lot, and to my surprise, wow! Everything he was wearing matched in color. He looked like a model in a magazine selling men's clothing. It was difficult to keep my mouth shut, but I did. I must be getting more mature; my mom would have been proud of me. God bless her soul. It took us about 1/2 hour to arrive at the club, and I was impressed seeing manicured grass, trees, etc., and a circular driveway to the front. As soon as we arrived, three to four employees took the boss' clubs and asked us what's going on. The privilege of being a member of a private golf club. Captain Flynn's clubs were placed on a golf cart and driven away. Forget that let's get us some breakfast. I followed him to a private dining room. I never saw so much food in my life for breakfast. I remarked to Captain Flynn that this was unusual. He looked at me and smiled. "Dean, believe me, when you become a member, you pay for everything in this place one way or another. As we walked into the room, the Chief of Police, the Mayor, Daren (the DEA boss), and a few others, who were strangers to me, were present. The Mayor gave us the usual salutation and asked us to serve ourselves. We took his advice and filled up our plates. Captain Flynn and I had one hell of a breakfast, and soon after the meal was over, we were escorted to another private room within a few minutes. The Chief of Police opened up by thanking everyone for their contributions. He explained the ongoing operation to all contact personnel from each area for about an hour. In closing, he gave Captain Flynn a very nice compliment on his planning, as usual. The Chief asked for any comments, only to have the Mayor get up and thank everyone for their professionalism. Looking at his body language, he could not wait to talk to the press. Lastly, he said, "Ok, thank you everyone. Let's play some golf! Everyone moved out quickly, and we were escorted to the golf carts. Each player was placed into their cart, and off they went. I waited for all of them to move, and my golf partner was Lieutenant Max. We just looked at each other and followed the game. As the day went on, I was impressed by how nice everyone looked, very color coordinated. All I heard all day long were two very prominent phrases: fore and mulligan. I didn't have any idea what they were talking about, but every time they said those words, they all chuckled and continued playing. It went on for a long five hours, but at least I was not on a boat. Lieutenant Max and I talked about everything, and I realized he was a good guy in a tough job. It was fun looking at all those folks looking for a little white ball all day long. Finally, Captain Flynn was finished, and we both got in our cars and went home. The only remark he made was, "Dean, I am really tired and can't wait to go to bed. We both finally have something in common, sleep." On my way home, I kept on thinking that maybe I should not be so critical and join the golf world. All I need are clubs, fancy duds, and learn how to say fore and mulligan. That should not be hard, and by the way, I would also have to learn how to smoke cigars. Not really. That's not me, and I don't have any patience.

I called Scott for an update. An hour passed by the time we connected. Nothing unusual; everything seemed normal around the Bolero, but he remarked that the staff were very low key and there wasn't much movement by anyone. The only important remark was that our boy Cooper was planning a trip to Panama. "How did you hear about that?" "He was at the club a few days ago when I overheard a conversation with the manager of his Panama trip. I guess he needs a vacation." "Thanks, Scott, be careful." I surprised myself and watched TV until 11:00 o'clock, and as soon as the news was on, I fell asleep this time, but I slept in my own bed.

To my surprise, Captain Flynn called me around 10:00 o'clock in the morning and asked me to meet him in his office. At 1:00 o'clock, he was right to the point and seemed a little uptight, so I figured operation whatever the Mayor was to call it was a go very shortly and I was relieved to get it over with and watch the outcome of all this planning and investigating that was ongoing for close to a year and a half. I am drained, and I need a change. Mary and I have been talking about a nice, quiet vacation. We are really looking forward to one. As I arrived at the station, Captain Flynn was waiting outside the building. He just got in the car and told me to keep driving. He explained the complete operation with only six locations from Scott's list. I asked him why only six? He explained that once the complete list was made available, the DEA started to have a 24/7 watch on all of them and felt that these are the top units that can produce the results we expect. He also, in every detail, explained who was at headquarters and in charge, including himself and all other members. Sergeant Scott will be the floater in case new situations arrive. Without causing any leaks, I would be assisting Lieutenant Max, who is assigned to the detention center because they have all the service areas for such a large operation and all detectives will be assigned to Lieutenant Max. Once the employees start to come in, he will give them the go-ahead to start the questioning, but not until all deliveries from GI imports are completed to the assigned stores. When all employees are ready to open the door, that will be the clue for every unit signed to the store to move in. Sergeant Lisa's expertise will help us move all the employees quickly and as quietly as possible to their cells. One very important topic of conversation was that the personnel involved must surrender their phones for one day until everything is secured, and all communication will happen strictly through the police phones only. "Captain, some of these topics didn't even cross my mind." "Dean, that's why I get the big bucks," and for once, he smiled. "I will call you and just say 'Miami', and that's when you move your position quickly. Now, get me back to the office. My last meeting will take place with the command group tonight. I will leave you a message to be on standby. Get yourself some rest because you will need it." "Have a good night, Captain."

I drove home and just hunkered down with my pizza and TV to try to relax. The call-to-action password had to come from the Mayor. It's just his flamboyant style. God help us! I did not get much sleep last night; anxiety, apprehension, nervousness, and fear, all came into play. Finally, the phone rang. I waited for the message and just heard a quick few words. Tomorrow is going to be the longest tomorrow in my life. No wonder my hair is starting to grey. I just need more sleep, but I was just too nervous to go upstairs, so I did the next best thing. I picked out my clothes and laid them out like I was getting ready for my first dance. The craziest things go through your mind when you get nervous. After this thing is over, the first person that mentions the word "Miami," I will for sure choke them. Finally, D Day arrives, and I have been dressed since 6:30 in the morning. One hell of a dance I'm going to. I hope I remember how to dance. Suddenly, the phone rings, and I wait for the message. False alarm! It's only my mechanic reminding me about my oil change appointment. I just started laughing. It really calmed me down. I took my jacket off and tried to relax. I looked at my watch, and it was 11:45. Where the hell is my call? It's bathroom time again. No sooner did I put on my pants, the phone rings, and the message is nice and clear: Miami. I almost tripped while getting to the door of my car, and off I went, driving a little faster than usual. But who the hell cares! I headed to the detention center. I met Lieutenant Max and Sergeant Lisa and just hoped for the best. I grabbed a cup of coffee and started to hear the chatter of the units, so fear was good. I felt better when the first group arrived. Finally, they arrive with bewildered people not knowing what the hell is going on and why they were in this situation. Slowly and quietly, they all gather in the sectioned area. They were supposed to wait there until detectives speak to every one of them; until then, they were instructed to relax. Lieutenant Max calls all the assigned detectives and explains their mission to them. They are similar to the instructions given in any other potential drug bust; only this time, it's on a larger level. We continue to interview them until we make sure that everyone's paperwork is complete for future evaluation. Sergeant Lisa's staff will be outside the interview room to escort them back. Sergeant Lisa instructs her team, "Just be very careful and complete your usual routine. Grab your coffee cup and get ready. It's going to be a long day and possibly a long night. Good luck to all." The chatter continues on police radios, and another group approaches the detention center. Everyone is slowly processed and escorted to their assigned rear area in the center. Lieutenant Max gives the go-ahead to start the interviews. I can see that with this many people, it's going to drag out. With two groups of employees, we accumulated at least 40 people. I can imagine to what size the total number of people could add up. This place is bustling with voices, remarks, and activity, but the police chatter continues. I hope the inspector comes over after completion of the sweep and gives us some evaluation, but it's still a long way from that point. Lieutenant Max and I start to take a peek at the interview on site. Everyone is looking concerned, and it's up to the experience. You can start to sort out the real ones from the fakers; it's a tough job. Sergeant Lisa and her staff are really terrific at personnel control. You can tell they have great experience. They take the day slowly and continue as expected. The distance is from store to store; that is the reason that the personnel delivering are taking more time to reach us. The most important thing is that everyone involved is safe. An hour or more passes, and another group is here. I can tell it's a new wave of people talking, and it seems that this batch is a little smaller;

but that's just my opinion. Lieutenant Max is going to reach out to some of the completed interviewees and just talk to the guys to get their opinions. Another hour goes by, and Lieutenant Max returns. I anxiously ask, "Any luck?" "Potentially a few fakers are there in Group A. It's a good sign."

It's nearly 1 o'clock in the morning and the last group has just arrived. The chatter has toned down and that is a good feeling for all the officers so far, no injuries, etc. As soon as they were delivered, they were gone. Great job and great teamwork. It makes you feel good to be able to serve the community with professionalism and pride which have always been our #1 goals. The police chatter has finally stopped, and I can just imagine what is going on with the command staff. We are informed that Captain Flynn and the Chief of Police are on their way here for some sort of update. As usual, it's a waiting game now. It's around 3:00 o'clock in the morning, and finally the brass shows up. Everyone looks tired, stressed out, and partly glad that the sweep is over. They call the available officers to the main office and explain to them the situation. Overall, everything went smoothly; only a few employees ran and could not be apprehended, but it was successful. Captain Flynn asks, "Lieutenant Max, why is this operation going very slowly." "Sir, people are scared, concerned, and overall confused."

"It's going to take at least two days to fully process everyone. Release the workers and hold on to the fakes." One detective asked what the overall drug quantity was. "We have not received the total amount from the DEA squad yet, but on the surface, it is a large quantity. The Chief of Police jumps in, "Let me answer that question. We have to make sure we get this right. No theatrics, just facts. Our biggest problem right now is making sure that Mayor Alvarez does not start a press conference before all the facts are completely sorted out. Every newspaper and TV station is standing by the Mayor's office like a bunch of wild dogs. To keep it calm, we have assigned plainclothes and uniformed police personnel; hopefully, the first press conference will be later today. So, for now, thank you for doing a great job. Keep the TV on and try to get some rest, if that's possible. In the meantime, Dean, we want your input on the interview process, where Lieutenant Max will provide the latest update. If I may, let's give everyone, a full hour's rest and then continue with the interviews." "Ok, I will inform them."

I was asked by Captain Flynn to get a headcount that we can supply. He says, "By the way, when we are ready for the press conference, I will advise both of you when to report to the Mayor's office." "Yes sir." Both of us could not sleep or rest, even if we tried. Our motors are in a high gear, and it's very difficult to slow down. We both needed another cup of coffee, and both of us lost count after ten. We will need sleep again, eventually. All of us meet in the conference room, and it looked like a bunch of college students trying to recover from an all-night bar hopping event—not pretty! Four hours seemed like a few minutes ago. We have no idea what in hell is going on in our minds. I need to stick my head under a very cold faucet to maybe bring me back to reality. The interviews continued and all seemed well. We received a phone call from the committee to be at the Mayor's office by 5:00 o'clock sharp. We both smelled like dogs and needed a shave and a quick shower. Sergeant Lisa gave us both some soap and shaving cream. We tried to look decent, and we both sprayed a can of deodorant on our clothes. We smelled like Lily of the valley! We made it to the Mayor's office, and the Chief was correct; it looked like a circus. Thank God for our saving grace, our police badges. Finally, inside the Mayor's office, there is a complete group of dignitaries. We felt like the bad boys of a World Series championship team. They looked at us and wiggled their noses. Lily of the valley made an impression. We looked at each other and smiled. In all of my life, I never saw so much newspaper and TV coverage. I just tried to look like I belonged, and we both hid at the very end of the group. Mayor Alvarez looked really fine for the occasion and thanked everyone for their attendance.

CHAPTER 14

"LADIES AND GENTLEMEN, I WILL EXPLAIN THE SITUATION AND inform you about the raid that took place today. When I took office a year ago, as part of my responsibility, I promised all the voters of our great city that I would respect and protect every single person in our fair city. All of us have been reminded by the media of one of our greatest problems: drugs. In our city today and here by my side, the people who, for the past two and a half years, have made it a first priority, along with your Mayor, to keep us safe. The Chief of Police will now give you a breakdown." "Thank you, Mr. Mayor. Let me start by explaining as much as possible to all of you about what took place. Personnel from the DEA, FBI, and Miami Police's special investigation unit were spread across the city for the past two days. Their targets were six local pizza shops that not only sold pizza but were the largest fentanyl distributors throughout our fair city. We, at this time, have arrested over 60 people, who are being interviewed. I just want to inform their families that they are all well, in good spirits, and will be returned shortly after being cleared by the special investigation units. We do not have a total fentanyl map as of now, but I can assure all of you that the quantity is well above 40 pounds, which has an enormous dollar value on the streets. The most important part of all this is the potential life savings for our community." "Thank you, Chief." Ladies and gentlemen, I cannot, at this time, answer any of your many questions that I am sure you have, because I am still going through the investigation, and we don't want to tamper with the work that still lies ahead for our team. I have been assured by them that at our Friday

10:00 o'clock meeting here, no question will be left unanswered. Thank you." They were furious a news conference with no real substance; they slowly left the packed room, and I could tell their disappointment.

The group was slowly directed to another room, and as soon as all the news media were totally cleared, the Mayor gave the ok to bring everyone drinks. We really needed them. He was assured, always clean, and, as usual, he went to the head of the class. "First of all, gentlemen, let me thank all of you for a great job." "By the way, Mr. Mayor, that was kind of close." "Raise your glasses and drink; we have two announcements that I am sure all of you will appreciate." "Takeover, Chief." "For the past eight years, Lieutenant Max has been on the Captain's promotion list. For your info, his name, along with six other candidates', were passed on in this year's list, and with only a single opening, it was a very tough choice to make. But I am pleased to announce that he was chosen unanimously. Lieutenant Max, or should I say "Captain Max." The group started clapping like crazy. "Come on up, Captain." Lieutenant Max looked shocked, and his eyes were very glassy. He just kept rubbing them. As soon as he got to the front, everyone just swarmed to congratulate him. You can tell that he was happy. He slowly caught his breath and could speak happily. He finally got his composure and thanked everyone in the room, and he just repeated "I never thought that this would ever happen. Well, I can't wait to tell my family, please give me a double." Everyone just laughed. After a few minutes, the Mayor says, "For the next announcement, let me call up Captain Flynn." He slowly moves to the front, and it seems as if he choked up a little. "First, let me just say that this individual has been one of the most improved and hardworking officers. In my personal project, he and his great crew were a very important part of our success." He starts to choke up and says, "Let me call up Detective Dean and personally give him my original Lieutenant badge, which

was given to me by his father many years ago, our own Chief
Dean." The crowd went crazy, and I could not believe that this
was happening to me. I started crying, and my knees got weak. It
seemed like an eternity to get to the front of the room, and I just
not could not help being overwhelmed with emotion. My face
was wet, and I just hugged Captain Flynn and could not give a shit
that I was crying. I finally got my composure together. "Never in
all the ten years on the police force I considered that this was going
to be possible. Captain Flynn was my driving force. He believed
in me. It was not easy; he pushed me every day. Thank you, boss.
I hope my father is looking at me with a smile on his face. The
second person I want to thank is Mary, my beautiful girlfriend.
Without her, none of this would have happened. Gentlemen, I'm
going to get drunk." They really started laughing. Somebody
screamed, "Don't get too drunk, Mary is in the Mayor's office."
The Mayor thanked everyone, and the meeting was over. Slowly,
I got out the door, and Captain Max was waiting for me. "Dean,
you worked your ass off on this project for a very long time.
"Max, there were a lot of good people who really helped me along
the way." I finally got to the Mayor's office, and Mary and Dana
came over and congratulated me. Once everyone left the room,
Mary and I hugged and kissed, and tears started to run down my
face. "Mary, did I ever tell you that I love you?" "Dean, you're
drunk. I will drive us home."

The next day, both of us got up, and I started making breakfast.
A few minutes later, Mary walked into the kitchen. "Good
morning, Lieutenant." We just hugged and kissed, and she turned
on the Morning News. Local news flash: On Saturday, Morning
News was informed by our station's local Coast Guard that, as
of this morning, a small Cessna was observed in the horizon
having engine trouble and exploded as the cutter reached the area.
They managed to recover two bodies; no further information is
available at this time.

ABOUT THE AUTHOR

Joseph Grande, author of Second Chance, is a father of five, husband of 60 years, and veteran. Born in Cuba, Joseph and his mother departed to New York City where they spent his youth in Hell's Kitchen, Manhattan. As a young man, Joseph enlisted in the military and began his 25-year journey in the Army and Navy. Joseph now resides outside of Philadelphia with his wife. In his free time, he can be found golfing and spending time with his family including his 10 grandchildren and great grandson.